Dancing In the Rain

(The Italian Family Series)

Lucy Appadoo

This book is dedicated to my mother, Antonietta who inspired the events in this story that is a work of fiction. I am honoured to have my mother in my life and for guiding and supporting me throughout my life. She is a true inspiration.

Contents

Chapter 1

FARM LIFE - 1963

The mild autumn weather was perfect for planting wheat. As the wind waved Valeria's fringe into her eyes, she wiped her brow with the back of her hand and then shovelled a hole two inches deep and spread the fertiliser. She scrunched up her nose at the strong odour, then scattered the seeds into the prepared area. The final touch was covering the wheat seeds with soil so they wouldn't dry out.

Valeria smiled to herself. She was excited she was to be growing wheat for pasta and bread to sell. It was her family's livelihood to work on the farm in her hometown of Laurino, in the southern part of Italy. She liked the farm and the nearby village, but wished she could see more of what lay beyond it. She didn't travel much outside the region of Campania, and what she knew about the villagers in her town, she'd learned from those who liked to gossip. Elderly women sitting outside their small homes watching people walk by. If something unusual happened, these women reported the incident to anyone and everyone. It hardly mattered whether the story was true or not. Events became twisted. Assumptions were made. If a woman spoke to a man, the gossipers would assume he must be her boyfriend. Who needed reporters when you had the villagers spreading their mishmash of truth and lies? It was one of the things Valeria didn't like about the village.

The braying sound of the donkey behind her jolted her as she took off her working gloves and turned. Her mother was tugging the donkey towards her, the green in her mother's eyes brightening further with the daylight sun.

Valeria's eyes were the same green, and she had the same slim frame. Her family had started telling her she was getting tall, though she knew she was only of average height, but she could almost look straight into her mother's eyes. The thought made her smile again. She was almost a woman.

She stood up and brushed off her skirt, then smoothed the auburn hair that fell to her shoulders in waves. Between the dirt and the sweat, she must look a mess.

Her mother looked at Valeria's neat rows and smiled. "Good work, Valeria. We'll have a great wheat harvest. Now we can bring the olives and get them pressed."

Sacks of olives lay on the donkey on either side. Valeria grabbed on to the donkey and pulled him along, while her mother took deep breaths and wiped the sweat from her eyes.

"Mama, I can't wait to make our own pasta, bread, and rice to grow. We can have a feast."

Her mother gave her a sad smile. "Maybe at least once a year we can have your feast, but with today's economy we are lucky to even survive. We must be grateful for the rewards of our hard work." Her short, petite frame looked overpowered by the donkey but her mother pushed on, tugging at the cross around her mother's neck.

Valeria was prepared for the long walk to their house, and didn't mind taking in the mountainous views, the blue skies, and the deep valleys ahead.

Her arms ached halfway through the trip but she carried on because she couldn't disappoint her mother. She swallowed as she wondered whether all of this hard work on their farm was worth it.

Her parents worked hard for measly profits as she knew the rich got richer and the poor got poorer, but she was excited when they reaped the rewards. They had all their needs met on the farm with the cattle they maintained for their milk, the grapes they made into wine, the pigs they killed for the sausages and prosciutto, as well as the cannellini beans, corn, figs, cherries, apples, and pears they produced. Yes, they were blessed to have food that kept them healthy.

Valeria passed by a young girl who wore nice clothes, jumping rope in front of a bigger house. Her heart sank. What she'd give to be able to have fun and do something different. She was fifteen now, becoming a woman, but sometimes she wanted more out of life. Wasn't it her right? She knew she should feel honoured to help her family, and she loved them deeply. She just wished she had time to do other things.

Walking down the hilly slope with her left hand pressed into the donkey's strap, she viewed her house in the near-distance. The soles of her feet ached, and she looked down to notice the holes on the sides of her shoes. She needed a new pair especially for these walks, but her mother said they couldn't afford it at the moment. She'd need to wait until they sold the olives.

They finally approached the village centre of Laurino, strolling past the butcher, a medical clinic, clothing store, pasticceria, and a statue of soldiers from World War 1, then the soccer field and church. She loved looking at the shrines built into the walls, a memorial for the deceased, as they continued down the narrow walkways and arrived at their house.

Her mother tied the donkey to the post then unlocked the heavy timber door. She entered with Valeria following. Loud voices resounded in her ear as her sister, Carla, grabbed her by the hand and asked, "Where are the olives?"

Valeria shook her head. Carla who was the oldest at sixteen, always cut to the point. Rather than saying hello, she was all business. Her tall stature made Valeria feel small at times. Carla stepped back with an expectant smile and toyed with her brown waves.

"They're outside. Papa and Emilio can get them. Where's Elena?"

Carla pushed past her through the door, then came back in. After a moment, she said, "In her room reading, I believe."

Valeria watched her father talking to her mother in the small kitchen that featured a rectangular table, small bench space, and a wood fire oven. Pots and pans hung above the bench but they were rusty and old. The weathered crockery looked ready for the trash heap, but their small portions of food always tasted delicious. She salivated just thinking about their simple, yet tasty foods made with organic, home-grown vegetables.

Her father frowned and raised his voice. "Why in hell couldn't you bring the olives inside? Do I have to do everything around here?" He pushed his stocky build away from the table, his black eyes even blacker as he nodded to Valeria, then rushed outside for the olives. His brown hair had a tinge of grey that hadn't seemed so obvious months ago.

Her father came back inside, then called out to Emilio, who came out of his bedroom. He was short but largely built and strong for his nine years.

"Coming, Papa." He laid a hand on Valeria's shoulder and smiled, showing his dimples.

Valeria smiled back, then walked into the bedroom she shared with Carla and Elena. Emilio had his own tiny room. Both rooms were cramped, so Valeria had to share a bunk bed with Elena, which wasn't the best. Carla, being the oldest, had her own bed.

Elena sat on Carla's bed, reading one of her school books. Valeria sometimes wished she could've stayed in school but her parents needed help on the farm. Most likely, Elena and Emilio would have to leave school sometime soon too.

"Hey, Valeria. What's happening?" Elena asked.

She shrugged then sat beside her sister on Carla's bed." Just planted the wheat and brought down the olives. You know, the usual stuff that you don't do."

Elena laughed. "Ha ha, you're funny." She touched Valeria's shoulder. "Well, I go to school and work just as hard as you do."

Valeria smiled, thinking that for an eleven-year-old, Elena always had an answer for everything. "Sure you do." Valeria turned at the sound of footsteps then waited for the explosion she knew would come.

Carla held her hands across her waist with pursed lips. Her face was bright red. "How many times do I have to tell you both not to sit on my bed? You have your own, so move it."

Elena sighed. "Here she goes again."

Carla leaned in towards Elena, staring her down. Then she grabbed her by the arm and shoved her towards the bunk bed.

"Come on, Carla," Valeria said. "You know we don't have much room there. Can't you be a bit flexible for once?"

Carla pressed her hands against the top blanket of her bed, then turned to Valeria. "Both of you need to take more responsibility. Even Papa says that."

"Papa—." Valeria said, then closed her mouth.

"Papa what?"

Valeria looked at Carla. She wanted to say that Papa was more controlling than Carla but she couldn't form the words. She wondered if she'd ever find her voice.

"You guys need to stay off my bed."

Elena climbed on to the top bunk and read. Valeria looked away and lay on the bottom bunk bed. Then Carla spun on her heel and left, still in a huff.

Chapter 2

THE SLAP

Valeria's mother called her and Elena in for dinner. She rose from the bed and nudged her sister who was deeply engrossed in her book. Eventually, Elena rose and climbed down the ladder of the bed, stamping her feet on the ground.

Her parents were standing in the centre of the kitchen by the sink, inches from each other, speaking intensely. As they walked into the open space of the living area and the kitchen, Valeria heard her parents' voices rise. A muscle in her father's jaw twitched. An anxious feeling settled in her stomach. Her mother gave her a nervous smile.

Her father said, "Are you laughing at me?"

Her mother shook her head, but looked away.

Valeria drew back, a knot forming in her throat. Then his hand shot forward, grabbing a fistful of

Mama's hair. Teeth clenched, face tight, he squinted down at her as if daring her to move.

Mama stood quietly, her head bowed, blinking back tears. She closed her eyes, then opened them and said softly, "Please, not in front of the children, Enzo."

Her father's other hand suddenly flung hard across her mother's cheek. The sound of the slap made Valeria gasp. Hairs on her arms prickled and her heart raced.

Elena yelled, "Papa, no! Leave Mama alone. What are you doing?" She threw herself between them. Papa gave Elena a hard look then moved to the table.

While Valeria hugged herself, rooted to the floor, Elena wrapped her arms around their mother, ushered her towards the living area, and sat her on the bench. Valeria stared at her father. He dropped into his chair with such force the rice spilled out of the bowl. Ignoring the rest of the family, he grabbed a spoon then took a sip of his rice soup.

Eventually, Emilio, Carla, Elena, and their mother came to the table and sat down. Her father's slurping sounds made Valeria ill, so she turned away and watched the stony expressions of her siblings and mother.

Valeria swallowed and joined the family at the table. She wasn't hungry, but the soup warmed her body, which felt cold and numb. The silence was unnerving, so she broke it by telling the others about her wheat planting. "I can't wait for all the nice things we'll get from the wheat," she said to no-one in particular.

As if she hadn't heard, Elena turned to her father. "I can't believe you did that to Mama."

Papa shrugged. "Well, if a certain someone had done what I had asked her to, she would've preserved her dignity."

"But Papa, what did Mama do?" Elena asked. Surely, she didn't deserve to be slapped."

Carla added, "Papa, we can help you and Mama more if you like. Mama works hard, very hard."

He slammed his fist on the table. "Stop it! Both of you. This is none of your business."

Elena stood up, her bowl almost toppling over the table. She held out her hands to make her point. "Well, if it's your business then why do you slap Mama in front of us? That doesn't make sense." She swallowed. "This is our family, and what happens to Mama is our business."

Valeria waited for the explosion and as she expected, it happened.

Her father abruptly rose, leaned in towards Elena and yanked her long chestnut hair. "Do you wish to be punished too, Elena? Is that what you want?"

Elena's lips quivered. "I'm sorry, Papa. Please let go!"

He let go of her hair, then turned towards his plate and finished his soup. He grabbed a chunk of ciabatta and spread homemade butter on it as thick as cheese. The rest of dinner time was spent in silence. Her mother kept her eyes on her plate while Valeria picked at her food, frowning.

Her mother had never stood by any of them. She always let him get away with his bouts of anger and mood changes.

Shouldn't the family be protected from a man who was always angry? Someone who constantly had something to complain about? Why couldn't her mother ever stand up for herself? Why couldn't her mother be stronger?

Valeria suppressed a pang of guilt. Yes, her mother was nurturing and a great listener, but Valeria needed more from her. She wanted her mother to protect her from a man who never listened and who liked to bully his family. He couldn't get away with this. She had heard about this kind of thing happening often in other places, and how people wanted it to be against the law. She knew that, in Italy, the police didn't get involved in private matters, but she felt that her father should be punished for treating them this way. Maybe one day, those laws about violence in the home would pass here, but would her father be alive to see that? Would she?

Valeria drew out of her thoughts and helped to clear the dishes. Her mother's cheek was bruised, and when Valeria touched her shoulder, her mother brushed it off. Mama turned to the sink in silence, gripping the plates and scrubbing the dishes hard. She slammed the plates onto the dish rack, and her hands shook as she handled the cutlery. It made Valeria's chest hurt.

Her father called out to her. "Valeria, go to the pasticceria. Here's a list, and come straight back."

She grabbed the list with shaky hands. "Yes, Papa." She gave her mother a hug from behind, then dried her hands and grabbed some liras from her father. Rushing out the door, she was glad to be out of the thickness in the air.

She took a deep breath and stepped onto the cobbled ground, clutching the money as she passed the other stores. Women hung clothes on their balconies, their underwear flapping in the breeze for all to see, and men sat in front of their arched doorways smoking their pipes. Wasn't there a better place to poison the air instead of affecting all the passers-by? She held her breath, then exhaled to avoid breathing in the toxic fumes.

She strolled past the butcher and a clothing store, then came across her best friend, Alessandra, from school. They had seen each other as often as they could, now that they had been out of school for a while, but Valeria missed seeing her friend every day.

Smoking a cigarette outside another clothing store, Alessandra looked up with a smile and leaned in for an embrace. "Oh, my dear Valeria. Long time no see. Where have you been, my dear?"

Valeria shrugged. "Busy with the farm, you know. Just like you're busy with your aunt's sewing business." She suppressed a flash of envy. She loved to sew and would give anything to trade places with Alessandra.

Alessandra threw her head back, laughing. "That's a joke. I keep pricking my finger trying to sew her damn pieces, yet she still gets me to do it. I might as well go back to school, or one of these days, I'll probably stab myself to death with one of the damn needles. Who needs it?"

Valeria stopped herself before she could say she needed it, and shook her head instead. "Well, you never did like school either, so what do you like?"

"Not much. Maybe one day I'll figure that out." Alessandra looked into the distance, seemingly distracted for a moment. "Oh yeah, boys. I really like boys."

Valeria turned to look behind her and saw a boy standing in front of a house as if he was guarding it. "Who's that?" she asked.

"That's Ciro. I've been seeing him for a while." Turning her eyes away from him, Alessandra said, "Listen, why don't we get together on the weekend. Hang out in the centre, what do you say?"

"Depends on my father. He's in a mood."

Alessandra chuckled. "Isn't he always? Just sweet-talk him." She blew the boy a kiss, then licked her lips as if teasing him. Valeria felt sick, watching her flirt with him. She was too young to be acting that way. If Valeria behaved that way, her father would literally kill her.

There were also things she liked about Alessandra; her fiery spirit, her courage, and her strength to tell people exactly what she thought. She even loved her bright red hair, similar to her own, her deep, hazel eyes, and her tanned skin.

"Okay, well wait for me at the usual place then."

Alessandra nodded. "Anyway, I'd better go see him. He doesn't like to be kept waiting."

Valeria grabbed her hand. "Wait! What are you doing with him?"

Alessandra gave her a cheeky grin. "Things you could only dream about, but don't worry. He's pretty good to me. See you later."

Valeria felt an emptiness in her chest. She stared at her friend, wanting to trade places with her for even one day. The freedom, the carefree attitude, and the courage to go after what you wanted. She wanted that, and so much more.

She hugged her friend goodbye, then watched as she ran over to the boy in front of his home and planted a deep kiss on his lips. The boy squeezed her breast. They set off through the narrow path. Where were they going, and how could she behave like that in front of all those women who loved to gossip? Maybe it was because Alessandra's father didn't care much what she did. If Valeria acted that way, she'd be as good as dead.

Chapter 3

A BEATING

Valeria bought the items on the list from the pasticceria but didn't head back home straight away. Her body felt tired as she played over the slap in her mind. She didn't want to be scared of her father. It was silly not to have the will to return home. On the other hand, why should she want to go back, when all she'd get was a mother whose head hung low, quiet siblings, and her father ranting and raving about all the things they did wrong? It was never his fault, always someone else's, but if she was to defy him, things would only get worse. He was not a man you disobeyed or answered back. Poor Elena always tried, but eventually he'd hit back at her and she'd crawl into her shell. Then she'd forget about the incident and do it all over again. Valeria admired her little sister's tenacity and courage, knowing full well what he was capable of. In spite of suffering after responding to his bullying, Elena always managed to continue her fight. Emilio did his best too. If only he was older, he might've had some measure of control over their father.

Valeria paced to the city centre, briefly nodding to women who sat outside their homes to watch passers-by. No doubt they'd talk to her father about watching her walk towards the city centre when she should've gone straight home.

Valeria headed to the amphitheatre where she had an open view of the mountains and valleys, a shade of greenery and slivers of brown across the landscape. She drew closer to the partial artwork the amphitheatre presented then stared at the statue of soldiers from World War I. The area was crowded, with some people taking photographs while others chased children inside the spiked fence that enclosed the statue. She spotted a tour group walking around the town square while the guide explained the history of the artwork and the statue of soldiers. Muffled voices behind her made her turn, and her heart skipped a beat when she spotted Alessandra chasing her boyfriend in the opposite direction. Why couldn't she behave more appropriately? Didn't she know that people around this village had nothing better to do than talk?

Continuing to watch them run off, she finally saw the boyfriend catch her friend. He lifted her dress, but Alessandra pushed his hand away. They disappeared around the corner of the building, but Valeria was sure she would hear about it from one of her mother's friends.

Making her way back through the near-darkness, Valeria sighed and wondered what she'd find. Would Elena be bringing the household to life as she usually did or would her father yell at her for not coming straight home?

Her feet stepped through the narrow paths. When she arrived home, she took a deep breath and braced herself. Opening the heavy door, she only heard quiet and realised it must've been later than she thought.

Her father sat on the bench, and turned abruptly. His teeth were clenched and his face appeared more wrinkled than normal. Even his body seemed to shake uncontrollably. He moved towards her. "You're home awfully late." Was he still mad at her mother? Why did he look so angry? He rubbed his hands together and took deep breaths, glaring and taking a step closer. The veins in his temple looked as if they were about to burst. "Why are you home so late, Valeria?"

She shrugged. "I—I just went for a walk."

"Do not lie to me." He drew closer to her, his eyes darkening.

He stepped in close, then raised his right arm and slapped her hard across the cheek. She lost her breath, and touched the sting on her cheek.

She moved back. "What did I do, Papa?"

Without warning, he flung himself towards her and shoved her onto the bench. In one quick action, he lifted his jumper and took off his belt. He swung it towards her, but she jumped back, and the strap whooshed past her shoulder. Her hair lifted on her nape and arms, her hands clammy. She had to get away. He was a madman.

In a heated frenzy, he chased her around the room. The buckle of the belt struck her arms, her breasts, and her legs. It felt like knives cutting her skin. Finally, cornered against the bench, she crouched into a tiny ball with her arms protecting her face, and her eyes closed to shut out the pain. When she opened them again, the room seemed to spin around her. Her father was a blur, a monstrous shadow, and her arms and legs were slick with blood. Her body shook, and her arms felt heavy. She couldn't stop him even if she tried.

His voice broke with rage. "You dare betray me! And with a boy!"

Valeria looked up at her father, at the dark coldness in his squinting eyes. She trembled, her heart pounding. "What boy? I wasn't with any boy, Papa. You're mistaken."

"And you still have the nerve to deny this?" He gripped the belt and swung it towards her chest, her hands, and towards her face. She covered her face with her hands, deflecting the blow. Her body froze. She was drained, and her body had had enough. She sank lower into the bench, defeated.

Abruptly, he stopped. She looked up, as Carla pushed her father away and snatched the belt from his hand.

Where was her mother?

"Papa, stop this!" Carla cried. "What is going on here?"

Her father pushed Carla aside. "Do you want some of this too?"

Valeria lay on the bench, sobbing with pain. She'd bled all over Mama's cushions, but she couldn't seem to make herself move. Instead, she clenched her teeth and closed her eyes, trying to think of another time, another place. Anywhere but here.

Carla shook her finger at him. "You're my father, but you're not my boss, so stop this! Tell me what happened."

Her father's voice sounded far away. "Giovanna came here and told me that your sister was with a boy. No doubt they were kissing. It's a disgrace, such a disgrace to this family. A dishonour to me and all I stand for."

Valeria swallowed but stayed down on the bench and peeked through her fingers when she heard her sister speak.

"That's ridiculous. Valeria would never do such a thing."

Her father glared. "Giovanna knew what she saw, and she believed it was Valeria."

Carla held her hands across her waist, sighing. She glanced at Valeria, giving her a reassuring smile. "Papa, Giovanna likes to gossip but this time she got it wrong."

Valeria felt Carla's warm hands around her, but her whole body ached from the touch. She shook her head. "No, leave me alone."

"Darling, let's get you to the laundry and wash your wounds. It's okay."

The front door swung open, and as Valeria slowly sat up, she turned to see her mother's stricken face. She rushed to Valeria and hugged her gently. "What happened here?"

Her father stared into the distance. "Your daughter is a disgrace to this family. Giovanna saw her running around, kissing a boy behind our backs. She is no longer any daughter of mine."

Her mother held up her hands in protest. "No, Enzo. I talked to Giovanna. I'm sure she had it all wrong."

Valeria stood up, ignoring the pain. "No, it was Alessandra. She has a new boyfriend. I just took a walk into the town square after going to the pasticceria. Giovanna was mistaken."

Her mother, Graziella, stared at the ground, shaking her head. "Just a case of mistaken identity, Enzo."

Her father grunted. "Still, she should've come back home just as I asked."

Carla stared coldly. "But Papa, she didn't deserve to be beaten with your belt."

He rose from the table. "I'm going to bed. Good night!"

No-one responded as he stomped out of the room. Valeria's lips trembled and her insides felt like they'd explode. How could he just walk away without an apology? He had no courage to say he was mistaken, always putting the blame on others. This was all wrong. He shouldn't always get away with it.

Her mother and Carla washed some face towels and pressed them onto her hands, chest, and face. Valeria felt tears sting her eyes as the warm water intensified the pain.

"I am so sorry, darling," her mother said. "He shouldn't have done this to you."

"He didn't even apologise, Mama. He was wrong and couldn't even admit his mistake." Valeria watched her mother's face pale and her eyes lower.

"He has had a hard life, Valeria. A very hard life."

Carla's eyes flashed. "That is no excuse to be violent towards Valeria."

"No, it isn't, but let me tell you a story," her mother said as she dabbed the towel to Valeria's face.

Chapter 4

MEMORY LANE

G raziella cast her mind back to the time she'd first met Enzo. She looked away as she told her story, her heart broken. "I first met your father at a family dinner." She closed her eyes briefly. "He was charming and a true gentleman. I still remember that little dimple when he smiled. Just like Emilio."

Enzo had asked her father for her hand in marriage after he'd known her for only two weeks. He had showered her with gifts and flowers, and treated her like royalty. "My princess," he had called her, and his eyes had shone when he looked at her.

They'd always met with her family around, so they didn't spend much time alone until the day they were married a few months after their first meeting. Still, she fell deeply in love and was ready to be his wife.

As she told the story, she wondered what had happened to that man. Had she really known him? Or had his experiences changed him to the point of no return? His mother had died when he was two, and his father was a mean, arrogant, and cold man who never said a kind word to anyone. She and Enzo had stayed with him on the night of their marriage. After they had made love, they fell asleep, but in the middle of the night, her father-in-law burst in. He said, "Get up and tend to the fence. It needs fixing and the sooner you get it done, the quicker we can keep the animals safe. Now get up! Don't let me tell you twice."

Enzo quickly got up and forgot about his wife. He didn't apologise for his father but left her alone in bed without a word. For many nights, he was interrupted by his father wanting something fixed or tended to. On one occasion, when Enzo had said he was tired, his father had pounded him in the face, then grabbed him by the ears and hauled him outside. Finally, his father had remarried and moved to Canada, and Graziella was grateful that they'd never see him again. Yet her trouble was not over, for Enzo had started turning into his own father. The man she once knew no longer existed, and in his place was a different man, someone cold and hard. Or perhaps that man had always existed but it had been dormant all this time. She wondered if she'd done something to awaken the anger inside him. Maybe she could've got him help to deal with the trauma of his upbringing. There must have been more she could do for the man she'd fallen in love with. She sometimes still saw a glimpse of his gentle side and knew it was within reach somewhere inside him.

Looking at her daughter's cuts and bruises, Graziella felt sick to her stomach. This shouldn't have happened. She would readily have taken a belting for her dearest Valeria, but she was afraid for her headstrong daughter. How could she help Valeria understand her father? Knowing that he had a sweet, warm side to him. How could she help Valeria find that side?

"I make no excuses for your father, but he never had any good role models. His uncles were hard and mean, and his father always put him down. He had little confidence and felt unloved by anyone from an early age. I know it's not right what he's doing now, but I think he needs to know that we love him."

Valeria wiped the tears with the back of her hand. "I don't love that monster. I never did, Mama."

Graziella took her daughter's bruised hand and stroked it gently. "Darling, you must learn to forgive. We must all learn and understand where he is coming from. As a family, we must respect him as the head of the family."

Valeria's eyes widened. She turned away with a shake of the head, avoiding Graziella's eyes.

"Why did you let him slap you, Mama? He can't get away with that."

Tears burned Graziella's eyes. She could not explain to her own daughter that a part of her was scared of Enzo. She had to be strong for the sake of her family, and put up with whatever her husband dished out. She had no choice. How would they survive without him? How would she cope?

She imagined the possibility of being divorced, but dismissed the idea. She needed to keep her family together. It would be shameful and a disgrace to be divorced. That could simply not happen.

Besides, she still loved him, though she didn't always like him. Maybe in time, he would come to understand, and that gentle man she had fallen in love with would return. For now she would do what she could to protect her family, and that meant she had to obey him and keep the peace. She would never let this happen again. She'd bear the brunt of his violence if it came to that. She respected Enzo, and knew he had his good side, and she could help him be the old Enzo again.

When Valeria's wounds had been tended and the girls sent off to bed, Graziella slid into bed beside her husband, who was snoring. She watched him sleep and wondered if he even felt loved. The anger he held inside him was surely directed towards his father; the ridicule, the taunts, and the chastising over the years. Wasn't that the source of his anger? Wasn't it also about the lack of control Enzo felt he had when his father had ordered him around constantly? He never found a way to channel that anger in healthy ways, and now he projected it onto his family.

She remembered Enzo telling her about his childhood. At one time, he had shown his father a drawing he was proud of. His father had said, "So you think you're an artist now, do you? What a load of rubbish that is! Put it in the bin."

Then she remembered how he had cried when Emilio was born. The pride and honour he felt at having his own son. She had to help him find himself.

Graziella awoke to a loud knocking on the door. She groggily rose, not wanting the others to wake up. Rushing to her feet, she put on a dressing gown and answered the door. When she swung it open, she was surprised to see Alessandra bursting in.

"Hi, Mrs Allegro, I need to speak to Valeria. Is she awake yet?"

Graziella lost her breath, knowing what Alessandra had been up to. She wondered if Alessandra's adventures would get Valeria into further trouble. "It's very early, dear, but I'll go check. Wait here."

Graziella went into her daughter's room. She lifted the blanket off her daughter and realised she was awake. "Valeria, Alessandra would like to speak with you."

Valeria covered herself with the blankets, her eyes dark. "Tell her I'm still asleep."

Graziella stroked her cheek. "But darling, why? She obviously wants to explain about yesterday."

"No, Mama, I don't want to see her. Please send her away."

Graziella resigned herself to the situation, then walked back to Alessandra. "I'm sorry, but Valeria's still sleeping."

"Can't you wake her up? I need to apologise about yesterday. My papa told me what Giovanna said, and he wasn't very happy about it. Please let me speak to her."

Graziella touched her on the shoulder. "I'm sorry, dear, but she needs her rest. Perhaps comeback tomorrow."

Alessandra looked like she was about to cry. She started to turn away, then hesitated and said, "Was Valeria punished last night? By her papa?"

Graziella felt a twinge in her stomach. How could she respond to that? She couldn't tell Valeria's best friend that because of her, Enzo had beaten her violently with his belt.

"Don't you worry about Valeria. She will be fine, dear."

When Alessandra left, Graziella closed the door and leaned against it. She wept silently, vowing that next time, if there was a next time, the pain of the belt would be on her own skin, not her daughter's.

Chapter 5

SOCIAL WITHDRAWAL

Valeria lay awake the next morning, staring up at the ceiling. She covered her ears at the snoring sound Elena made and pulled the blankets higher. Her body felt cold and she ached all over, the bruises still raw. She looked at her hands and saw dried blood in the beds of her nails and the creases of her skin. She touched her swollen cheeks and winced at the sudden searing pain.

Valeria couldn't stop the shakes and felt a deep emptiness in the pit of her stomach. She turned over to her side, not wanting to face the day, and heard muffled voices. It was the sound of her parents' voices in the next room.

How could she ever talk to her father again? Why had he hit her without even talking to her first? She never had the chance to tell him the truth. He listened to gossip but couldn't be bothered finding out if it was true or not. How dare he listen to Giovanna, and take her word as more important than his own daughter's? What gave that woman the right to get involved in other people's affairs? She had no life, that's what it was, and because she had no life, she felt the need to destroy a family with her unfounded accusation. If only she could give that woman a piece of her mind, but what good would that do?

Giovanna would continue to gossip about other people because that was the type of woman she was. An old-fashioned lady who had lost her husband and was now estranged from her children. A woman so miserable with her own life that she had to make others miserable. Well, she had no right. No right to cause Valeria's father to attack her so brutally, to wound her very soul, and lose any crumb of trust she had in him. How could she trust her own father again? How could she trust anyone?

She forced the thought from her mind and steeled herself for the day. Then Elena's voice sounded in her ears.

"I'm going to school, Valeria. Are you getting up?"

Valeria shook her head and covered her face with the blankets. She couldn't face Elena. "No, I'm staying in bed."

"Are you okay? Mama will be calling for you to work today."

"Tell Mama I'm not feeling well, will you?"

Elena dropped to the floor and yanked the blankets abruptly off her sister. Valeria turned away and covered her face with her hands. Elena grabbed her face and turned it towards her. Her mouth dropped open, and the blood leeched from her face. She stared hard at Valeria. "What happened? To your face?"

Valeria pulled the blankets back over her trembling body. "Nothing. I'm fine. Just get ready for school."

Elena stood cross-armed. "I'll do no such thing until you tell me the truth. Now tell me!"

As Valeria pondered her words, Emilio rushed in like a hurricane towards Elena. Carla followed him behind but stayed silent.

"Aren't you ready for school yet, Elena? Hurry up." Emilio turned towards Valeria, his eyes widening as he headed towards her.

"Why have you got bruises over your face? What happened?"

Valeria frowned, watching Carla closely. "Come on, Emilio," Carla said. "Valeria needs to rest today. She's not well."

Emilio turned to Carla. "But I want to know, what happened to her face? Was it an accident on the farm?"

Valeria's stomach hurt. "I accidentally bumped into the door last night, nothing major. Now get ready for school."

He stood cross-armed with pursed lips, his eyes piercing. "I'm not stupid. What really happened?"

Carla grabbed him by the hand. "Let's go, Emilio. This is not the time. Valeria needs rest. She's not feeling the best, so let's go."

Emilio leaned in and pecked her on the cheek. "I love you, Valeria."

As they both headed out, tears stung her eyes and wet her cheeks. She was blessed to have a family that cared for her, but how would she get through the coming days?

Valeria forced the tears away and quivered under the blankets. Looking at Elena made her insides sick. She knew how deeply her sister felt things, and admired her tough spirit, but right now she just wanted her to go away.

Footsteps drew closer and her mother entered the room, prodding Elena. "Darling, get ready for school and have your breakfast. Please go!"

Elena left the room, shaking her head. Her mother came close and wrapped her gentle arms around Valeria. "How are you feeling today?"

Valeria's chest felt empty. "Fine, Mama."

"I spoke to your father and he's okay with you staying home today. No need to come to the farm."

Valeria chuckled. "Well, so nice of him to let me stay home after what he did to me."

Her mother stroked her hair and looked her straight in the eye. "He feels terrible about what he did. Telling you to stay home is his way of saying he's sorry. He's a proud man, and you know his story, darling. He still has a lot to learn in the way of love and feelings, but he does love you, Valeria. Very much! He will one day learn to show that to you in more obvious ways. For now, we must be patient."

"For how long? He had all these years to learn, and he has learned nothing. I don't think his history should affect his treatment of us."

Her mother looked away for a moment. "No, you're right, but it defines him. In time, I believe he will be more understanding—more open with his feelings."

Valeria's throat felt dry. She was lost for words.

Her mother stood up, then leaned in and kissed her. She gave her a reassuring smile and walked out.

Valeria looked over at the empty bed and wondered if Carla had already left for the farm. She'd hustled Emilio out before he could press Valeria for more information. *I'm not stupid*, he'd said. How much did he know? Had he heard anything from last night?

Swallowing, she turned over on her side and let the tears fall. She didn't bother wiping them away, and cried into her pillow. She ignored the pain spread throughout her body.

Her eyelids drooped. She felt tired all over again. Her body ached all over, so there was no way she could do physical work. Even tomorrow, she'd need to take it easy until her wounds healed.

Chapter 6

PREPARING A FEAST

A week later, Valeria returned from the market after selling boxes of pears, apples, blackberries, wine grapes, chestnuts, carrots, garlic, and beans, which were all in season in the autumn.

Valeria and her parents headed back to the farm to store the remainder of the supplies, as her mother planned to prepare for a feast with the fruits and vegetables harvested on the farm.

Carla, Emilio, and Elena were waiting for them outside the shed and all of them smiled at seeing the stockpile of the remainder of the supplies; those that hadn't sold at the market. After each special season, they liked having a feast and sharing food with their neighbours, family, and friends. It was the reward of working diligently for many months.

Valeria averted her eyes every time her father looked at her. Her bruises were still tender, the cuts just beginning to heal. Every time she looked at her wounds, it reminded her of what he'd done. She only spoke to him when he spoke to her so the remainder of the time, she avoided talking to him and imagined he wasn't even there. She could see the hurt in her father's eyes but she didn't care.

Valeria started setting a trestle table, hefting it with the help of her brother and sisters. They carried it over to an area that didn't get much wind. Then she added a weathered plastic tablecloth and thin napkins and cutlery. Finally, she placed glasses at either end to hold down the tablecloth. Elena and Emilio were staring at her, silent.

She stopped and frowned. "What's with you lot?"

Elena shrugged. "You're still looking terrible, but at least your bruises are gone."

"Covered with make-up," said Carla.

Emilio hovered over her, grabbing her hands, which were suddenly shaky. "I still want to know what happened to you." He looked over his shoulder at Papa. "Please tell me the truth, Valeria. I should know." There was shame in his eyes, but it wasn't his shame to bear. Again, Emilio turned towards Papa, squinting as if he was blinded by the image. His hands fisted for a moment.

Valeria took in the view of the landscape surrounded by vast greenery, the darkening sky shrouded with grey clouds, and fell silent. Cows they owned for the sale of milk grazed in the distance while trees rustled as if they were about to topple.

She could never tell her brother the truth. He was too young to know about such things, and she didn't want him hating her father. Emilio had a decent relationship with him. How could she threaten that relationship? It was between them, and had nothing to do with her brother. No, she would never tell him.

Emilio seemed to accept her silence as he took her in his arms and played with the strands of her hair. Then Elena joined in the embrace while Carla looked on. When the table was set, she smiled then left. Carla could be loving in her own way but was never the type to show affection.

An hour later, Valeria sat on the bench and watched a community of old men, women, and children bustling about as they strolled down the dirt path.

Women held trays of food, and men carried bottles of wine and plastic glasses to share in the feast.

Her father shook all their hands and kissed the women's cheeks, then nodded over to Valeria to do the same. She greeted the neighbours and her mother's sister and family, then joined her mother who was in the shed preparing pizzas. Taking a potato, she began peeling and slicing it while her mother spread the pieces over the pizza. When it was complete, Valeria placed the pizza into the stone oven made by Enzo. A warm glow surrounded her as she lingered near the oven. She looked up as her mother approached and touched her on the shoulder. "I'll be back, darling. Can you put these toppings on this pizza?" She pointed to the various toppings contained in dishes. "I'll say hi to everyone then I'll be back. I'm sure some of the signoras will want to help."

"Okay, Mama."

Valeria rolled up the sleeves of her jumper and washed her hands from the dirty potatoes, then added the cheese, garlic, mushroom, and peppers onto a prepared pizza dough. She added a touch of olive oil, then put it in the oven, feeling the heat rush to her face.

Turning back to the table, she started rolling out the dough, kneading and pressing into it with the palms of her hands, feeling the stickiness on her fingers. She dabbed flour onto her fingers then looked up as a figure appeared in the distance. She squinted and tried to make out his features. They didn't get a lot of strangers here.

He walked up with a swagger and gave her a smile. "Hi, I'm Giovanna's son, Gregorio. I'm from Tuscany and I've come to stay awhile." He held out his hand. Valeria stared at it, then wiped her hands on a dirty tea towel and shook his hand. It felt cold and hard. His hand lingered for a moment too long. An uneasy feeling washed over her. She noticed his bushy eyebrows, protruding chin, and stocky build. In spite of his large frame, he looked rugged and slightly handsome, with dark eyes and rakish grin.

She couldn't believe she was meeting Giovanna's son, of all people. The woman who had spread the rumour about her. She wondered if he knew what his mother had done, but if he'd recently arrived, she doubted he'd know anything.

"Can I help with the pizzas?" he said, drawing closer. "They smell great."

She moved back a step. Her stomach felt rock-hard and her hands were clammy. She shook her head and returned to her kneading. "I'm fine. I'll have help soon."

His eyes turned serious, and he nodded. "I'll leave you to it then. I thought I'd at least introduce myself."

"Sure," Valeria said.

As he left, she felt that all of her energy was sucked back in. She got her breath back and wondered why he would leave Tuscany to come to Laurino. From what she'd heard, Giovanna's children had never wanted anything to do with her. What had changed? Why was he here now?

Chapter 7

UNEXPECTED VISITOR

G raziella watched Enzo clink glasses with their neighbours who sat on either side of him at the table. His hands flailed as he talked politics then took a huge bite into the potato pizza, wincing from the steaming heat. He was such a charmer around friends and not at all like the bully he was at home. How could she be a better wife to him? She had always tried her best to make him happy, but it seemed there was no pleasing him.

Graziella sat at the table and dipped her ciabatta bread into olive oil. She popped it on her tongue, enjoying the saltiness of the bread and the olive aroma of the oil. It was their own pressed olives made into homemade oil, and she couldn't be prouder. So much to be thankful for when working the farm and reaping the fruits of the harvest. She looked around at her family and friends and saw her daughters, Carla and Valeria talking. If only they could afford to keep Carla and Valeria in school. The skills they learned there could set them for life, but at least they'd do well in farming and domestic duties. Valeria was also skilled as a dressmaker but she didn't have much time to tend to the machine these days.

Feeling a tug on her shoulder, Graziella turned as Gregorio dropped onto the seat beside her. He gave her an absent smile, then his gaze slid over to Valeria. She felt unsettled as his eyes pored over Valeria who was happily laughing with her siblings. Why was he staring at her daughter? He'd better not have any intentions. She wouldn't stand for it.

Graziella cleared her throat. Quickly, he looked her way and smiled. "It's great to see how hard you've worked for all this food," he said. "It is quite the king's feast. Thank you."

Graziella nodded. "It's a pleasure." She saw something unnerving in Gregorio but she couldn't quite figure out what it was. "What brings you to Laurino? You haven't been here in a while."

His face flushed. He looked down into his lap and bit on a piece of garlic bread. "I thought Mama might need some help. She's getting old, you know."

Graziella nodded. It sounded reasonable but something in his tone suggested there was more to it. She didn't like the way he suddenly turned on the charm.

"But your mama's managed quite well on her own for all these years."

Gregorio shifted in his seat, then poured himself a glass of homemade wine. "I know she has, but can't—can't a son visit his mother for a while and tend to her needs?"

She watched him closely. "I suppose you're right." She met Valeria's eyes, a sombre look expressed on her daughter's face. "Well, it's good to have you here. It's nice to know your mother has help."

Gregorio didn't respond. His gaze was fixated on something behind her. When she turned, she was surprised to see Alessandra looking gaunt and white-faced as she approached Valeria. She seemed to hesitate, but then called her name. Graziella shook her head.

As much as Alessandra was a wild child, Valeria seemed so lonely without her. They'd been friends for many years so she couldn't expect their friendship to suddenly die. Besides, Alessandra had many good qualities and could be a good influence on her daughter in other ways. Alessandra had helped her daughter be more confident, and she had a good heart. Graziella would support whatever Valeria decided about the friendship.

Turning back to Valeria, Graziella felt sympathy towards Alessandra as her daughter pulled away and turned back from her. Alessandra's chin quivered, and her voice rose.

"Please, Valeria. We need to talk. "Alessandra stood by Valeria's side, trying to gain her attention, but Valeria refused to look at her.

Valeria's body stiffened. "No, we don't."

Alessandra bowed her head. "I'm sorry. I didn't mean to—"

Graziella drew back when Gregorio suddenly rose. She looked at the guests, who had suddenly stopped talking, their eyes fixated on the girls. He stamped over to Valeria and Alessandra, quietly introducing himself. Then he moved Alessandra aside.

"I'm Gregorio, a friend of the family's. Why don't we leave Valeria for now? Just come with me."

Alessandra shook her head. "No, I need to talk to my friend. Please!"

"I understand, but you're causing a scene. Everyone's watching. Come on, let's take a walk. Now's obviously not the time."

Gregorio flashed her a smile and took her by the hand. Graziella frowned. He moved Alessandra away from the guests and towards the dirt track.

Graziella watched with growing concern as they disappeared from sight but no-one else seemed to care. They didn't know Alessandra.

Soon enough, they delved back into conversation while Valeria looked stricken and played with her food, withdrawing into herself.

Graziella went over to Valeria. She comforted her daughter then sat back at her table. She looked around, realising Gregorio hadn't returned. A few minutes had turned into ten minutes. Her stomach turned. She had a bad feeling about this. Rising from her seat, she spoke to a woman beside her about returning soon, then made her way towards the road.

She headed out of their farm property and towards Laurino, where Alessandra lived. She heard the sound of her feet against twigs, stones, and the dirt path. The raspy wind brushed her face as a dark feeling surrounded her. She tried not to imagine what was going on.

A flock of birds flew overhead and she spotted a crow near her foot, but she ignored the bad omen. Surely, Gregorio was taking Alessandra home in good faith.

Running towards the narrow path, she was almost out of breath but carried on, hoping to reach them. Why had she let Gregorio go away with Alessandra? What had possessed the girl to come all this way just to speak to Valeria? Couldn't it wait until they returned home?

Stamping her tired feet against the blades of grass, bypassing trees and sloping surfaces, Graziella swore she could hear footsteps in the distance. If only she'd brought a torch in this near-darkness. How was she supposed to see where they were?

Muffled voices sounded in the distance, and as she stepped up her pace, the sounds became closer. It was like a silent cry that was surrendering, and she felt her heart almost fall out of her chest as the worst thought possible entered her mind. No, they couldn't be.

Rushing towards two figures up ahead, nestled against the trunk of a tree, Graziella cringed and braced herself. Gregorio was lifting up Alessandra's dress and kissing her hungrily. Alessandra showed her wild side by groping him in between his legs as his hands fondled her breast. His pants were pushed down to his feet.

Graziella used every ounce of energy to push Gregorio away from Alessandra. She snatched up a rock she spied near the tree. Holding it up to his face, she said, "Get out of here, and never come back."

Gregorio drew back, face reddening. He hurriedly dressed himself. "I'm sorry, but this was mutual. I didn't force myself on her. I only gave her what she wanted."

"Get out or I will tell Enzo what you've done. He'll have your head."

The fear in his eyes was evident as he nodded, staring hard at Alessandra, who was picking at her nails. After a moment, he made his way towards the city and didn't turn back.

Graziella's body shook as she turned to Alessandra. "How could you let this happen?"

Alessandra shrugged, her eyes lowering. Graziella stood cross-armed, her fists clenched. Her body wanted to explode. What did the girl think she was doing? Playing with fire.

Alessandra stood like a statue in silence, but Graziella gave her a piece of her mind.

"This is not the right way to behave, Alessandra. You are only fifteen. What would your father think about this?"

She looked up, her eyes narrowing. "My father?" She chuckled. "As if he'd care."

"But he's your father. Of course he cares."

Alessandra shuffled her feet, kicking the dirt as she avoided Graziella's eyes. She pursed her lips and sighed.

Graziella said, "I don't want you seeing Gregorio again. He is much too old for you and only has one thing on his mind. You must keep yourself pure, dear."

Alessandra lifted her head and stared hard at Graziella. "That, Mrs Allegro stopped a while ago. I am not pure, and my papa doesn't care."

Graziella felt sick, trying to process that detail. "If you promise not to see Gregorio again, I won't tell your father about this."

She shrugged. "Fine. "She scratched her temple. "Can I go now?"

Graziella nodded and watched Alessandra meander along the dirt path. The girl acted as if she didn't care about her life. Was she reacting to the way Valeria had pushed her away? Didn't she have any ounce of self-respect? Maybe having a father who didn't care made her behave this way. She was protecting her feelings. She didn't want to admit that she had felt rejected by Valeria when she also felt rejected by her father. It was a pure mask of self-defence. Graziella only hoped that Valeria would forgive Alessandra as her daughter might be the influence she needed to get back on track.

Chapter 8

THE TRUTH

As her mother returned to her seat and started talking to some of the guests, Valeria felt her chest tighten. Mama looked anxious. What was going on? Was it about Alessandra? She must've had a quick word with her, but Valeria didn't have the stomach to speak to her friend just yet.

Valeria was finishing up her meal. Her hand shook at the thought of seeing Alessandra. How could she ever forgive her for what she'd done? She'd wandered around with her boyfriend which led to Valeria's beating. It was partly Alessandra's fault, wasn't it? Didn't she know that people would think she was the same? Alessandra had to stop behaving like that.

Picking up a glass of water, Valeria drank. Looking around at the guests, she noticed that Gregorio had left straight after Alessandra. What was that about, and where was he now?

She rose as the female guests started helping out with the clearing of the table. Elena chased around another young girl while Carla dumped scraps of food for fertiliser, then scowled at Emilio and shouted at him to help. He was kicking a soccer ball around, but at Carla's shout, he stopped, shook his head and came over to the table.

Carla approached and nudged Valeria out of her dismal thoughts. "What's with you?"

Valeria looked up. "Nothing. Where did Mama go?"

Carla chewed at a piece of apple with such precision, intent on eating politely with her mouth closed. "She probably wanted to speak to Alessandra." She cleared her throat. "Listen, Valeria. You cannot blame her for what happened to you."

Valeria turned away. "I don't want to talk about it."

Carla shook her head. "Well, you're going to have to at some point."

Valeria didn't answer. She wasn't ready to forgive Alessandra.

The night air was fresh, their surroundings almost silent when Valeria and their guests walked back into the village.

When they arrived home, Valeria, Elena, and Carla ambled to their bedroom. Valeria and Elena fell onto their respective beds while Carla started brushing her long curls in front of the dresser mirror.

Valeria was dozing off in bed when her mother stepped into the room and nodded towards her with a concerned look. "Sorry to wake you, darling. Can we talk?"

"What about Papa?"

"He's listening to the radio in the kitchen."

Valeria forced her stiff body up from the bed. She hoped it wouldn't take long as she felt wore down from the day.

Her mother's room was scantly furnished with an armoire, a double bed with a cast iron bed head, and two weathered timber bedside cabinets.

They sat on the bed, her mother watching her closely. "Darling, I need to talk to you about Alessandra." She focused on the ceiling for a moment. "Can you tell me about Alessandra's father, and their relationship?"

Valeria wondered at such a question. Her hand fisted. "I don't want to talk about Alessandra."

Her mother looked away momentarily. "You can't keep blaming her for what happened."

Valeria sighed, wanting the conversation to be over. It was too late for this. "Why do you even care?" She felt her face burning and her body trembling, but she tried to ignore it and picked at a wine grape. It tasted slightly bitter with a hint of sweetness, matching her own sour feeling.

"I'm afraid she's going to get hurt. She's just a child like you, still learning, still growing."

Valeria had never given that any thought.

Her mother continued. "Tell me about her father."

Valeria pondered, wondering how much to share. "He—he works a lot, but sometimes he gets sick and stays home."

Her mother looked at her strangely. "What do you mean by sick?"

Valeria had wanted to share this with her mother, but Alessandra had forbidden her to say anything. A part of her didn't owe Alessandra anything, and another part didn't want to betray her. Now they were no longer on speaking terms, surely she was free to share. "He gets drunk a lot, so then doesn't go to work. I think he's lost a few jobs that way."

Her mother looked thoughtful, then shook her head. Her small hand rested on her chin. "Darling, does he even care what Alessandra does out there? With her boyfriend, I mean?"

Valeria angled her head. "I don't think so."

"And how long has he been drinking?" Silence. "Why on earth didn't you tell me this before?"

"Sorry, Mama, but she didn't want me saying anything. I had to respect her wishes." She sighed and continued. "He's been drinking since her mother died a few years back."

Her mother clasped her hands as if reciting a prayer. "Does he hit her when he drinks?"

Valeria thought of her father's pinched face as the belt rose and flung at her. She couldn't imagine Alessandra's mild-mannered father doing such a thing. "I think he just passes out."

Her mother rose from the bed. "I see." She drifted for a moment, then kissed Valeria on the cheek. "You go to bed, darling. I'll see you in the morning."

Valeria walked back to her room. Why had her mother asked her all those questions? Was Alessandra in some kind of trouble? She hopped into bed, and remembered when Alessandra helped her after Valeria had grazed her knee near the bridge. Then the time she helped her with Elena when her sister had bumped her head on the kitchen bench. She felt suddenly guilty for treating her badly. She promised herself she'd see her friend in the morning.

Chapter 9

INCIDENT

There was no opportunity to speak with Alessandra the next morning. Instead, her father took Valeria to the farm to tend to some errands while Mama and Carla were away. A group of men were gathering at the farm to assemble a new cowshed. They had all joined together to buy the supplies as the cows were cramped in their current shed.

The breeze was noticeably cool as Valeria flicked her hair into her eyes. She wished she was with her mother who was visiting a friend up in Bari. Carla travelled with their mother but only because her boyfriend was able to drive them to Bari, almost two hundred kilometres away.

Valeria watched men hammer nails into pieces of timber, saw wood, and use a ladder to start building part of the roof. Her father had wanted her to keep the men fed and hydrated.

She trembled in the cold and wore rubber shoes that felt too thin for the rough, uneven ground. She hugged her body, waiting for the men to be ready for their morning espresso. Her father rushed in her direction and pushed her towards the building housing the tiny kitchen. He looked at her through squinted eyes and sneered. "I thought I told you to make us coffee, not stand around and watch. Now go!"

Valeria drew back and nodded quickly. The familiar smell of dirt and mint always reminded her of her father. "I'm going. I'm going." She stamped towards the shed area, her day totally spoiled by her father's usual sour mood. Just once, she'd wished he'd be kind to her. Why was he always angry?

She entered the coolness of the shed and took a deep breath before setting out the coffee maker on the portable stove. She grabbed a rusty tray from the shelf, then shakily loaded minute coffee cups onto it. She put some sugar into a tiny bowl and the milk into a jug then some spoons resting on the saucers. Biscuits were laid neatly onto a plate, but she would have to bring them separately. Her father would most likely yell at her because she hadn't used her third arm to carry the biscuits. He always had to find something at fault, and it was never him. Oh, how she wanted to get away from him sometimes. His hair-trigger temper. The constant need to walk on egg shells. It was exhausting.

When the coffee was ready, Valeria poured it carefully into the cups then picked up the tray and set off towards the men, dodging the stray planks scattered across the yard. She hesitantly called out to them, "Coffee's ready."

Four men in caps and work boots gathered around her with warm smiles, grabbing their cups and adding sugar and milk. She hurried back for the biscuits and they wolfed them all down while her father ushered her to leave. As she turned, empty plate in hand, she spotted a spider almost as big as her hand emerging from a hole in the ground. She yelped and leaped sideways, stumbling onto a loose plank. A sharp pain shot through the middle of her right foot, and she gasped and jerked her foot up. The nail that jutted from the plank clung for a moment, then fell free, glistening with her blood. It had penetrated the arch of her foot. She looked at it more carefully. It was covered with rust, and the tip seemed to have broken off.

Valeria took deep breaths until her heartbeat returned to normal then steeled herself against the pain and limped back towards the shed. She glanced around for the spider, which was scuttling back into the hole it came from.

Her mother would be home sooner rather than later, and would help her tend to her wound. If she told her father anything, no doubt he'd blame her for stepping on it. She just couldn't cope with his complaint.

Valeria grabbed a cloth and ran it under warm running water then sat on a chair and rubbed her throbbing foot. Her hand pressed into the arch of her foot. It felt tender and warm with a tinge of red surrounding the sole of her foot. That couldn't be good, could it? Surely, though, she had time to wait for her mother. She rubbed her foot with the cloth then pressed hard into the wound to stop the bleeding. The pressure sent waves of nausea through her, but this should give her time to wait for help.

At the sound of footsteps, she threw the cloth on the floor and quickly stepped into her shoe. She heard her father calling her name. "Valeria!"

She turned to the voice. He entered, almost military-style with his stiff posture and cold, hard expression. "Make sure lunch is ready within the hour."

She looked up at him, his eyes the usual darkness, and she managed a smile in spite of her pain. "Give me some time, Papa. Are bread and peppers okay?"

He nodded. "Just make it quick. The men'll be hungry soon." He marched out and she felt the space clear up again. Quickly, she limped to the sink and grabbed potatoes stored in a side cupboard. She started peeling, wincing at the ache in her foot.

Valeria found some peppers stored in a box, then washed and popped them into a pan on the stove. With a hint of olive oil, she turned the peppers and cooked them until they browned and softened. The aroma of the peppers touched her stomach as she placed them on a plate. After cutting some homemade bread, Valeria put the peppers and bread on the table and, again, felt the pain. She was starting to feel a touch of heat in her foot. Her head felt strangely hot too, so she grabbed a glass of water and drank. Then with a slight limp, she went out to call the men and her father, who followed her back to the shed.

"Why are you limping?" her father asked as they reached the shed.

"Oh, nothing. Just twisted it the wrong way. It'll be fine."

The men sat down to eat and Valeria joined them but had little appetite. She picked at some bread and peppers, and watched the men devour the food as if they hadn't eaten for years. They talked about their plans to build another cowshed at someone else's farm, planning to chip in for supplies. It was a good way to save when your family barely survived.

She was starting to feel hot, so she drank more water. When the men finally went back to work, she settled at the table and waited before building enough strength to wash up.

When she started to stand, a pain sharp enough to make her cry out sliced through her foot and shot up her leg. She struggled to breathe and clenched her teeth. Then her father's voice cut through the haze in her mind. "The men want some more of those biscuits. Can you—" He stared. "What's wrong with you?"

"Not feeling so good, Papa. Feeling hot."

He grabbed her by the shoulder to hold her upright. He looked at her foot all swollen and red, and sat her down. "What happened?"

She turned over her foot. "I stepped on a nail in the field. I think a tiny bit of the nail is stuck in my foot. It might be infected."

His face paled and his hands shook. "Why are you telling me now and not earlier?"

Valeria curled into a ball and shrugged. "I thought—thought I—could manage."

He shook his head in fury. "Stupid! So stupid to wait this long." His hands were clenched. "Wait here! I'll get the donkey."

Valeria bent her head and closed her eyes, feeling hotter by the minute. She would get through this.

Chapter 10

MEDICAL ASSISTANCE

Enzo pushed the donkey towards the shed. How could his daughter be so stupid, leaving her wound untreated for all these hours? What was she thinking? She should have known this type of wound could be dangerous when infected, particularly with a rusty nail from the dirt. How could she put her life at risk like that? If only Graziella was here. He hated it when she left for these occasional visits. She knew better about these things than he did.

The thought of Valeria's pale, sweaty face made his stomach clench, but the fear quickly turned to anger. He had to punish her, to teach her she could never behave that way again. He wouldn't indulge her weakness by going with her. No, she had let the wound fester on her own, so she would see the doctor on her own. He had his job here to finish for the day.

Besides, maybe this would teach her a lesson and make her stronger. That was what his father had taught him; strength through suffering. Nobody but weaklings lived life any other way. Yes, this would teach her next time to ask for help immediately.

When he entered the shed, she was sitting in the corner, hands clasped around her knees. Tears streamed down her cheeks. The tightness in his chest and the sudden ache in his legs only steeled him further. Giving in to emotions would not teach her anything.

He took her by the arm and pulled her to her feet. She slumped against him, looking up through listless eyes, and another wave of anger surged through him. No daughter of his should be so weak. He pushed her weight onto her own legs and gave her a quick shake, then pulled her outside and grabbed the donkey's reins.

He moved the donkey closer to Valeria, then crouched and lifted her onto the donkey's back. She hunched over its neck, her fists clenched in its mane. Heat radiated from her body.

He grabbed a flask by the sink and filled it up with water. "Here, take this." He pushed the flask into his daughter's hands, then jerked the donkey along, listening to her slow, deep breaths. Oh, how he saw the potential in Valeria. She was smart and capable, a force to be reckoned with, and sometimes his love for her was so fierce he thought it might burst his chest. She had a wilful streak that couldn't be abided though. Like keeping her injury from him. As if he wasn't her protector, or as if he didn't deserve to be respected and honoured.

He pulled the donkey to a stop and turned to Valeria. "Now, I want you to go straight to the clinic in Laurino," he said firmly. "No stopping anywhere. Ask for the doctor and tell him exactly what happened. He'll help you. You'll be fine but don't make any unnecessary stops."

Valeria's eyes widened. "You're not coming?"

He pushed aside a pang of guilt, and another burst of fear and anger bubbled up inside him. "No, I still have a job to do here. The men need me. Now go! There's no time to waste."

"But Papa, it's such a long trip."

She looked so small, so frail. He almost relented, but no, that would only make her weak. "You'll be fine." He swallowed and gave the donkey's rump a slap. "Make sure you drink."

Valeria nodded in resignation, then pulled on the reins. At the change in pressure, the donkey turned its head and plodded towards the village.

The hilly, rough terrain made her wound throb as she slouched over the donkey. Her body shook with heat. Putting the flask to her mouth, she took a few sips and felt a little better.

Valeria couldn't believe her father would let her travel all this way on her own. How could he? What if something happened to her on the way? Did he even care?

She felt the softness of the donkey's back and patted it gently, watching a storm brewing. The blue sky was being overtaken by the grey clouds and the wind was picking up. Hopefully, she'd get to the clinic before it started to rain.

In the distance, she saw tiled roofs amidst rows of houses with green, towering laurel trees lined up in a straight fashion. The dark, green mountains loomed ahead, a jagged silhouette against the rolling dark, grey clouds. Other trees and shrubs sat in clumps around a multitude of homes and buildings in a downward slope. The church towered in the distance as Valeria realised she was getting closer.

She felt feverish so took more sips from her flask and wiped her brow as the donkey pressed on as slow as ever. Not long to go now, she thought. Just a little further.

Briefly closing her eyes, she thought about the comfort of her home and the way her mother would pray the rosary in church and at home, playing with the cross around her neck. She had a strong belief in the angels and constantly spoke about Archangel Gabriel, the guardian of children and Archangel Rafael who kept people safe on their travels. Valeria hoped they would protect her now.

Her breathing was becoming more erratic and her vision blurred. She bent further over the donkey as she passed into the village centre not far from the medical clinic. She took another drink and willed herself to stay upright on the donkey's back, then forced herself to push on, holding tightly to the reins.

She was dimly aware of people staring, but they looked like tourists rather than locals. At this point, she didn't care. Let them take pictures of her if they wanted. Just a poor little village girl hunched over her donkey.

Pressing on past the narrow walkways, she heard the nearing footsteps and faint voices getting closer. Were they calling out her name? She frowned, trying to clear her head. Were the voices even real?

"Valeria? Valeria stop!" She felt the arms of a young girl grabbing her by the shoulder gently.

"Are you okay? What happened to you?"

Valeria turned, blinking the sweat from her eyes. Alessandra stood beside her, her brow furrowed with concern. She leaned in and stroked Valeria's face.

Valeria tried to speak, but her mouth felt dry. Alessandra's image was becoming blurrier by the minute, and there was a blackness closing in around her.

Alessandra, she thought. She was angry with Alessandra about something. That wasn't right. A lump rose in her throat as she toppled sideways and swirled down into the darkness.

When she awoke, she was lying on some kind of mattress, smelling disinfectant mixed with cologne. She opened her eyes and saw a familiar-looking man with grey hair and blue eyes. His hands were clasped across his paunch, and he was smiling over her as Alessandra hovered behind him, a concerned look in her eye.

"Hi, Valeria," he said. "Welcome back. I've removed the foreign body and given you an antibiotic to fight the infection in your foot. I was just about to give you a tetanus shot. It won't take long."

She nodded and closed her eyes, waiting for the syringe to penetrate her skin. She hated needles, but this time it was necessary. Feeling a slight pinch, she regained her breath and opened her eyes again.

"You are so lucky to have made it on the donkey. If this was left for more than twenty-four hours, you could've died."

Valeria sighed. Then Alessandra helped her up and held her tightly. With a relieved smile, she said, "I am so glad you're okay."

Valeria smiled back at her friend, realising what a horrible friend she'd been. It wasn't Alessandra's fault that her father had beaten her with his belt. All of that responsibility lay on him, not on Alessandra. Valeria felt a flutter in her heart just thinking about her friend's genuine empathy and care.

Chapter 11

FRIENDSHIP REKINDLED

A lessandra pushed open the door to Valeria's house. Muffled sounds came from the living room, and when they followed the sounds of their source, Valeria spotted Elena lying lazily on the bench. Emilio bowed over a notebook with a pencil in hand. They both looked up with questioning expressions, then rose to greet her.

"What happened to you?" Elena said as she rose.

Valeria limped over to the bench and sank onto it, then lifted her feet so they could see. Closing her eyes, she took in Alessandra's soft voice.

"Valeria got her foot caught on a nail. It got infected so she saw the doctor and had a tetanus shot. She's fine now, just a little tired."

Emilio rushed to his sister. He gave her a tight hug. "Are you sure you're okay now?"

Valeria nodded, opening her eyes just as Elena turned and stamped towards the bedroom on her little legs.

Alessandra followed her to the bedroom while Valeria waited on the bench. *What was going on with her sister?* Valeria was the one who was injured so why was Elena suddenly so angry?

It wasn't like she had it hard. She got to live a simple, easy life, reading all the books she loved to read while Valeria had to entertain a group of men and work heavily on the farm, pushing wheelbarrows, carrying burlap sacks of olives, selling fruits and vegetables at the market, and breaking her back weeding or planting for hours on end. When did Valeria get the time to do the things that she loved?

Between her time at the farm and helping out in the house, she had little time to indulge her love of sewing and dressmaking. So what did Elena have to be angry about?

She came out of her reverie as Emilio gave her a kiss on the cheek and returned to his homework. A few moments later, Alessandra returned. She sat beside Valeria and took her hand with a reassuring smile.

"Elena's upset about things, that's all," Alessandra said.

Valeria pushed her body up with her right hand, wincing at the tenderness in her foot. "What kind of things?"

Alessandra blushed, lowering her head. "I'm so sorry what I did to you."

Valeria turned her friend's face towards her. "What does that have to do with Elena?"

Tears streamed down her friend's face. "She's upset about your father hitting you—and now this happening to you. She's worried about you, and hates to see you in pain."

Valeria nodded. "She's so sensitive. Things get to her easily, but she has to learn to toughen up."

Alessandra shook her head. "She's only eleven. How can you expect that at her age? I think you need to talk to her, reassure her that you're fine. Calm her down a bit."

Valeria took a deep breath. "I'll speak to her." She grabbed Alessandra by the shoulder, ignoring Emilio who was eavesdropping on their conversation. He was clever enough not to get involved.

"I'm sorry, Alessandra," Valeria said. "I was mean to you when it wasn't your fault. It was my dad's doing, not yours. He was the one who hit me."

Alessandra held back more tears, exhaling deeply. "But don't you see? If I didn't behave that way, you would've been okay. Giovanna wouldn't have spotted me and nothing would have happened."

Valeria turned away for a moment. "So why do you behave that way? You know that the women around here love to gossip. They have nothing better to do. We live in a small village so you've got to be extra careful."

Alessandra shrugged. "I don't know. I get angry sometimes, and I—"

"You what?" Valeria watched her closely, realising there was more to her friend's story. She might've had the freedom but did she have the care of her family? When Alessandra turned away, Valeria continued. "I'm here for you. You can trust me with anything. You've always been there for me, and I'm sorry. Know that you can confide in me—always."

Alessandra stood up and paced the floor, staring at her feet. She cleared her throat and pressed her lips.

Then turning back to Valeria, she sat back on the bench and fixed her gaze strongly on Valeria. "My papa doesn't care what I do. Ever since Mama, you know."

Valeria stroked her hand. "Then talk to him and make him get help."

She nodded. "I'll try."

Valeria flashed back to the feast they'd had. "I saw you leaving with Gregorio. Did anything happen between you?" Silence. "Alessandra, did anything happen? I saw Mama leaving the guests, and she'd been gone quite a while."

Alessandra blushed. Her hands fidgeted. "Please don't judge me."

Valeria's face felt hot and a sinking feeling penetrated her stomach. "And what about your boyfriend, Ciro?"

"He doesn't have to know. Besides, I'm not tied to him."

Valeria stared. "But there's something funny about Gregorio. You should stay away from him."

Alessandra grimaced. "I might. Your mama gave me a good lecture. He was just a bit of fun but I don't plan on settling down."

She gave Valeria a warm hug. "Listen, I'm going now. Please go talk to Elena. She needs you now."

Valeria nodded, looking at her friend with concern. Then she rose from the bench, ambled to the bedroom and saw Elena's head engrossed in a book on her bed at the bottom. She spotted Valeria and rose. "Sorry, I hope you don't mind me using your bed."

"No, it's fine." She headed over to her sister and pulled her into a tight embrace. "I love you, Elena, so much, but you don't need to worry about me. I'm tough."

She felt the wetness against her cheek, increasing by the minute.

Chapter 12

FARM HAND

V aleria's feet felt cold from pressing them into a large wooden crate filled with red wine grapes. She stamped her feet and held on to the edges of the crate as her feet turned blood-red, sinking into the soft, squishy sound of the pressed grapes.

Her mother, standing beside the crate, grabbed Valeria underneath her arms and hauled her out of the tub. Valeria stepped onto a dirty, damp towel and wiped her feet. They felt sticky, the broken skins of the grapes caught between her toes. Her mother hosed her feet down, and the chilliness and sharpness of the water made her gasp. She shivered and hugged her body as the cold breeze whipped her hair around her face. She suddenly felt clean, and smiled to herself at the freshness of her feet.

Valeria dried her feet with another towel she found hanging by a hook outside their shed. She sat on a smaller crate, dabbing at her feet, feeling the wind brush up against her bare skin. Then she slipped on her boots and went to carry crates of dried tomatoes to the shed. She placed an open crate at the end of the table and lined up a series of smaller ceramic jars. After grabbing a handful of tomatoes, she placed them into the small jars, then added oil and sealed them tightly.

As she worked, some of the oil fell on her hands. It felt soothing to her dry, chapped skin. Almost like a moisturiser. She looked down at her hands, roughened by the long hours working in soil and the open air. She wished she had soft, smooth hands like the girls in Alessandra's magazines, but there was nothing to be done. The garden had to be planted. The tomatoes had to be dried.

She sighed and continued on her task until she heard voices outside. She sealed the lid on the jar she was working on and headed outside.

Valeria watched her father strolling over to the partly made cowshed. He was working with the same group as last time but with one exception. Her chest felt heavy. Her mouth went dry as she saw Gregorio, with his swaggering motion and confident posture, laughing with the other men. What was he doing here, and why was he acting as if those men were his friends? He'd only been back for a little while and now he was acting as if he owned the place.

He was not a man she liked. Not after he'd taken advantage of Alessandra, a fifteen-year-old who didn't know any better. He did know better and he'd abused her in a way she didn't even realise was abuse.

Valeria sat on one of the crates by the shed and stretched with a yawn, tasting a bitter flavour in her mouth. Looking back at the group as they worked on the cowshed, she saw her mother approach them and shake her head. Then Mama moved over to Valeria's father and whispered something to him. He didn't answer. Instead, his eyes became slits as he leaned in towards Mama and gave her a shove, careful to avoid the watchful eyes of the others. Her mother cowered. Then, with her head down and her back stiff, she walked towards the village.

Valeria thought her mother was busy with the grapes but obviously, she'd come outside to share something with her father. Was it about Gregorio? About his relationship with Alessandra?

Moving back inside the shed, Valeria began storing the sealed jars of dried tomatoes on a shelf. Her wrists began to ache. She rubbed them gently and closed her eyes to hear the rustling sound of the strong wind outside. Then she sighed. Lingering didn't make the work go any quicker. Best to just get it done. Back on task, Valeria continued to put the jars away then cleaned the table. As she was washing her hands with hand-made soap, the sound of light footsteps made her turn.

It was Gregorio, standing behind her. "Can I help?" He gave her a broad smile and then winked.

"No, I'm fine thanks." She briefly turned back to rinse her hands under the tap. After a moment of silence, she turned off the tap and peered at him. "I thought you were helping out my papa with the cowshed."

He nodded. "I am, but we're waiting on some timber so I thought I'd check in on your work."

She swallowed. "I'm fine. I'm used to all this hard work on the farm. It's my job."

"Sure." He leaned in closer, licking his lips and fixating his eyes on her face. He stood quietly, staring.

She broke the silence, feeling uneasy. "How's your mother?"

He continued to stare. "She's fine. Never better. As fit as a horse, given her age. She's no longer that young but still works quite hard in the house. I try to help, but she doesn't have many years left. She needs to remember that. She has to slow down a bit, but she's as stubborn as a mule."

He reached over and touched Valeria's shoulder, stroking it gently. "Why don't you and me go out some time?"

Valeria stiffened. She shifted away from him and was about to leave when he moved in even closer.

He grabbed her by the arm. "Hey, don't go. Let's get to know each other."

She forced herself to look him square in the eye, refusing to let him overpower her. She could fight him if she had to. No problem! "I have an errand outside. I'm sure Papa will need you soon."

His eyes darkened. Then she rushed away, her elbows pressing into her sides as she pushed past him. She felt as if his dark eyes were boring into her back. She had to get away from him, and fast. The way he looked at her...

It wasn't right.

Chapter 13

RELATIONSHIP CONFLICT

The next day, Graziella trudged along the dirt path beside Giovanna, her arms hanging limply at her sides. She smiled politely to her companion and thought about this morning. Giovanna had banged on her door to ask Graziella to accompany her to pick up her son at the farm. Giovanna didn't like walking the long distance on her own, so Graziella had no choice but to take her. She wasn't sure about how she felt listening to Giovanna's nonstop gossip. Besides, it still hurt how she had mistakenly raved to Enzo about Valeria.

Her gaze wandered as Giovanna ranted on about nothing in particular. Suddenly Giovanna changed the subject, catching Graziella by surprise.

"I am so sorry about Valeria," Giovanna said. "I really didn't know it was her friend who was with that boy. Such a disgrace, though. To be behaving in such a way without any morals or values."

Graziella felt a sudden urge to slap the old woman. Instead, she smiled politely and picked up her pace. She pumped her arms and lengthened her stride until she heard Giovanna wheezing as she struggled to keep up.

With a pang of guilt, Graziella slowed her pace. Giovanna meant no harm. She had a sharp tongue but a good heart. Graziella must try to remember that.

The sound of an impending storm reached her ears, and she cast a worried glance at the gathering clouds. "It's okay, Giovanna. It was an honest mistake."

"But that friend of hers." Giovanna went on. "Should Valeria still be seeing her? I mean, with the type of influence that she can be—if she hasn't influenced her already."

Graziella's pulse sped and her muscles tensed. Heat flushed through her body. "Valeria's a great daughter with honour and values," she said, her voice tight. "Please don't think otherwise."

Giovanna knit her brows. "No, I didn't mean to imply such a thing. It's just that, well, Alessandra behaves in such a loose way, and to be associated with Valeria, well—you know."

Graziella didn't respond. They had reached the farm, thank goodness. Now she'd have some respite from the old woman's complaints. Giovanna was always so negative about everything and everyone. No wonder her children rarely visited. Did she ever look at herself?

Graziella had the sense that her companion was lonely and miserable, and maybe one day she'd question her about such things. For now, she'd leave it, but whether that was for Giovanna's sake or her own, she wasn't sure. She put on a bright smile and said, "Oh, we're nearly there. I can see the men working hard."

"Ah yes, I see. Such a long trip. I don't know how you do it every day. My Gregorio must surely struggle with such a journey."

Graziella didn't understand why Enzo had to invite Gregorio over to the farm after what he'd done to Alessandra, but the young man had promised to stay away from her. Apparently, Enzo believed him. Besides, whatever she told Enzo would be taken with a grain of salt. Her opinion never seemed to matter to him.

As they reached the farm, listening to the sounds of sawing timber, the hammering of nails into wood, and the crashing sound of roof tiles, Graziella saw Valeria holding out a tray of coffee and biscuits. She smiled, proud of the woman her daughter was becoming. Then the smile faded as she wished she could give her child a better life.

Graziella sighed. You could fill your basket with if-onlies and still have nothing but air. The simple truth was, they needed the extra help and couldn't afford to pay someone else. It was only through the generosity of their friends and neighbours, who pitched in with labour and supplies, that they were able to build the cowshed. They only survived through their social networks and hard work.

Graziella approached the men, Enzo, and Valeria while Gregorio gave a curt nod to his mother who grunted in response. He fisted his hands, then turned to the men.

Giovanna pulled her son aside and grabbed him by the ear. "What were you thinking, leaving the coffee in the pot? I told you to put the remainder in a glass and wash it, not just leave it there on the stove. Why can't you help out a bit more?"

His face blushed. "Sorry, Mama. I was in a rush to get over here and didn't have time."

She squinted and let go of his ear, leaning in towards him with an upright posture. "You know the rules when you stay in my home. You follow them or you get out. I won't be putting up with your stupidity."

He whispered, "Please, Mama. You're embarrassing me."

Graziella and Valeria watched the exchange turn tense when Giovanna's face distorted with rage. Without warning, she hit her son hard across the face.

"You dare tell me what to do? I don't know where I went wrong with you. You just don't seem to understand anything. How can you always be a good-for-nothing loser, always doing the wrong thing and making mistakes? When will you grow up and be a man?"

With a surge of pity, Graziella saw the pale colour of his cheeks as he looked down at the ground, his feet shuffling in the dirt. The men worked on in silence, but their eyes turned towards the conflict. Suddenly, Enzo shouted out, "Let's get back to work."

Enzo approached Giovanna and grabbed her by the hand. "Why don't you go and have a cup of coffee in the shed? That way, Gregorio can keep helping us a little while longer. We need all the help we can get."

Giovanna nodded and turned to Graziella who ushered her to the shed. "Let's go."

Valeria avoided Giovanna's eyes. Her posture was stiff and her face was tight as they walked off and left Gregorio, still stricken by his mother's outburst. Graziella turned and saw him smile at Enzo. Then he grabbed a hammer and banged hard, his teeth clenching. His rage seemed to come out of that hammer, but who could blame him? She suddenly saw a different side to Gregorio, and she felt sympathy for the man. How could a mother treat her child in such a devaluing way?

Chapter 14

DAY'S OUTING

Enzo sat on the bench, his feet resting on the small coffee table as he watched Valeria and Carla rushing in and out of the bathroom to their room, getting ready for a day out with Carla's boyfriend, Maurizio. His stomach sank at the thought of Alessandra joining them, but Maurizio was picking her up, so at least he didn't have to see such a person with so few morals. If it wasn't for Graziella telling him the girl agreed to behave herself in public, he wouldn't have allowed Valeria to see her.

The girl was a disgrace, and a bad influence on Valeria. He hoped she wouldn't corrupt his daughter to the point that she'd need another beating. He hated it when he had to discipline his family, but it was his job to be the strong one, to mould his children in the way they should grow. Heaven knew Graziella couldn't—or wouldn't—do it. A little bubble of anger pulsed in his chest. No wonder Valeria ran wild, the way Graziella indulged her.

He sank down onto the sofa. It was a Sunday, and he liked to have at least one day off from the farm. He let his family have a day of rest on Sunday. Later, he planned to listen to the radio and catch up with his friends at the coffee shop. Graziella would stay home with Elena and Emilio and somehow keep them busy.

Enzo pulled out his pipe and tamped a wad of tobacco into the bowl, then flicked his lighter over it and drew on the stem until the pipe was well lit. He leaned back on the bench, breathing in the strong fumes and letting them sink into his stomach. He looked up at the ceiling, pondering the work on the cowshed. That reminded him of Giovanna and how she had put down Gregorio with a passion.

It was a disgrace. Gregorio was a man and should have stood up for himself, not let a woman control him. Enzo's pipe suddenly tasted sour. He'd felt like slapping that woman, but he couldn't do that in front of the others.

Yet, she needed to be put in her place. Who did Giovanna think she was, humiliating her son like that? Enzo blew out a cloud of smoke, resolved to talk to Gregorio about acting more like a man and taking back his control.

Enzo's own mother had died when he was very young, but he liked to think she would never have treated him like that. He often wondered whether his life would've been different if his mother had lived. Would his father have been less bitter, more understanding? Would Enzo have had more control over his life when he and Graziella had lived with his father? He hadn't seen his father in many years, but a splinter of fear still settled in his stomach at the thought of the man.

The sound of Carla's voice jolted him from the bench. She came in and pecked him on the cheek. Then hesitantly, Valeria did the same. Her long face and the brusqueness of her kiss showed him she was still angry at him, but whatever for? Had he not cared for her when she'd hurt her foot? Was she still upset that he'd had to discipline her with the belt? How long could she hold on to such resentment?

Why should she hold it against him? It was that old busybody Giovanna who had confused his Valeria with Alessandra. He felt another rush of bitterness towards the old woman. She was a troublemaker, in such a hurry to share a bit of juicy gossip, that she'd accused his daughter falsely. His nostrils flared. It was wrong of Valeria to blame him. He had only done what any good father, any real man, would do.

Enzo turned to his daughter, Carla. "So, where's Maurizio?"

"He should be here any minute now, Papa."

He squared his shoulders and cleared his throat. "You know, if his father and I weren't such good friends, I doubt he would be your boyfriend. Is he treating you well?"

Carla nodded. "Yes, Papa. He is a true gentleman."

"So where are you going today?"

"Paestum, to see the ruins."

"And I guess that girl is going with you too?"

Valeria sighed and turned towards him, her head lowering as she spoke. "Alessandra and I are still friends, Papa. She is sorry for what happened."

Enzo grunted and watched Valeria closely. Her hands quivered, and there was a dullness in her eyes. He felt uncomfortable looking her in the face, but he chose to let it go. Now was not the time to discuss her disobedience and lack of respect towards him.

A knock on the door made their heads turn, and Enzo stood up abruptly, wanting to pay his respects to his friend's son. He swung open the door, smiled upon seeing Maurizio, and moved forward to shake his hand firmly.

"Maurizio, how are you doing?"

"Good, Mr Allegro. And yourself?"

Enzo ushered him inside, where Carla approached and gave him a chaste kiss on the cheek. Valeria nodded to him.

"Couldn't be better," Enzo said. He respected this young man as much as he did his father, and he trusted him implicitly with Carla. "So you're going to Paestum today?"

"Yes."

"Okay, don't make it too late. They'll need to be home by dinner time."

"Of course. I'll get them here, but you know it's an hour's drive from here. So we'll be gone for a while." Maurizio's eyes roamed the house. "Where are the others?"

"Oh, Graziella and the kids stopped by the shops. They'll be home shortly."

The young man nodded. "Say hello to them."

"I will." Enzo glanced at the clock.

"If you leave now, you'll have plenty of time to get back in time for dinner."

"Yes, sir." Maurizio stood, waiting for Carla and Valeria to grab their jackets. Then they all said their goodbyes to Enzo and stepped out of the house.

Enzo had an uneasy feeling about their trip with Alessandra. He hoped she wasn't bringing that boyfriend of hers. Even so, he trusted Carla and Maurizio to bring Valeria home safely. Although he remembered at first how he'd forbidden Carla to see Maurizio. She had daily arguments with him for months. It wasn't until Maurizio's father had convinced him, that he'd finally agreed to the match, and he now trusted the young man.

Chapter 15

NEW EMOTIONS

Valeria sat in the back seat of Maurizio's grey Fiat, sucking in a breath at the speed of his driving. Parts of Laurino whizzed by as he stopped at Alessandra's house and beeped his horn. The door flew open, and she hurried out, pausing just long enough to close the door behind her.

She slid into the back seat without speaking and pulled the door shut. Her brow furrowed with concern.

Carla asked, "Is your father home today?"

Alessandra pursed her lips, pressing the length of her palms against her skin-tight jeans. "He is, but he wasn't feeling well so he's in bed."

Code for being drunk, Valeria thought. She shook her head, grabbing her friend's hand with a reassuring smile, but Alessandra pulled her hand away and turned her gaze towards the window.

Valeria opened her mouth to ask what was wrong, then closed it again. Her friend's rapid breathing and stiff posture said she wasn't ready to talk.

Changing the subject, Alessandra said, "We're meeting my boyfriend, Ciro, and his friend Dario at Paestum. They're getting a lift from his father. Is that okay?"

Valeria's mouth went dry. Boys! Her father would kill her if he found out. She could still feel the sting of his belt against her skin.

Carla, in the front seat, looked back over her shoulder. "I don't know, Alessandra. This wasn't the plan."

Maurizio nodded. "That's right. Enzo wouldn't like this."

Alessandra lifted her chin. "I know, but he doesn't have to find out. Besides, you guys will be with us so we won't do anything you wouldn't want us to do."

Carla grunted in response, turning her head from side to side.

"This is a bit risky," Valeria said. Her throat felt tight and her voice lost some of its sound. She couldn't go through another beating. If Alessandra was wrong about this, that was exactly what would happen.

Alessandra smiled. "It'll be fine. They're great guys."

Shoulders slumping, Valeria turned away to focus on the passing sights of towering trees, large dirt tracks, and parts of the Cilento National Park before ending up at nearby villages, then Monteforte Cilento. She felt flat, pressed thin by the weight of seeing these boys. Why did her friend always take such risks? Was her home life that bad that she needed the distractions? Maybe it was.

She rubbed her damp palms against her thighs, then tucked her hands under her armpits and leaned her forehead against the window. Surely Alessandra would not risk compromising Valeria's reputation. Not after what had happened last time.

Somehow, she managed to force her mind back to the scenery and keep it there until an hour or so later when they finally reached their destination of Paestum, often called the Greek ruins.

Maurizio turned off the engine and they all exited the car and took a short walk to the site with its roofless ruins. Some of the grass on the ground was withered but in other parts of the site, the ground was freshly cut and a deep green.

Alessandra suddenly sprinted away from them, heading towards a short, muscular boy with a crew cut. Beside him was a lanky boy with curly hair that fell to his shoulders. Valeria felt a flutter in her stomach as the curly-haired boy walked towards them. Alessandra and her boyfriend followed from behind.

As they neared, Alessandra introduced them, her eyes roaming the area. "This is my boyfriend, Ciro, and his friend Dario. Guys, this is Valeria, my best friend in the whole wide world, her sister Carla, and her boyfriend, Maurizio."

Ciro leaned in and put out his hand. "Nice to meet you all."

"A pleasure," said Dario shaking all their hands, lingering in Valeria's. His emerald green eyes remained fixed on her face, and he gave her a warm smile.

Carla cleared her throat. "Why don't we go to the museum just opposite?"

They headed in the other direction, and Valeria rubbed her skin, a rolling feeling in her stomach. What was she so nervous about? Dario might've been a little handsome, and sure he was walking just a little closer beside her than was strictly necessary, but that was no reason for her throat to dry up and her brain to empty itself of all coherent thought. At least for now, he didn't say anything to her either.

They entered the museum and roamed the ground floor looking at the displays of sculpture and artworks. The tomb paintings from the Greek era gave her an unsettled feeling. She came out of her thoughts when Dario spoke. "I know a bit about these tombs. This is the fresco from the 'Tomb of the Diver'."

Valeria looked more closely at the picture, which depicted a man diving into water, then glanced around at the other tomb paintings. They showed scenes of fighting, hunting, and celebration.

"I just love Greek and Italian history," Dario said. "I'd like to be a historian one day or a history teacher."

She found her voice. "It sounds interesting. Are you still at school?"

He nodded. "I have two more years, and then I'd like to study at university. Maybe in Milan, and do historical studies."

"Good luck with that."

As he moved closer to Valeria, she smelled his heady scent of wood and cinnamon. It was a nice mixture, and his eyes remained fixed on hers. Again her knees felt wobbly. She looked away and pretended to look at some Etruscan artworks.

She spotted the others passing through the tomb paintings until they reached them. They headed to the ruins again, then stopped at a bar with outside tables and ordered lunch and drinks. As Valeria sat down next to Dario, Alessandra leaned in and kissed Ciro deeply on the lips, her tongue delving in deep. Dario cleared his throat and looked away while Valeria watched Carla shove Alessandra on the shoulder.

"Behave yourselves now," Carla said. "This is a public place."

Ciro grinned. "But she's gorgeous. I can't take my hands off her."

Carla sighed. "Well, try for today. My father doesn't know about both of you coming here, and he wouldn't be pleased about this."

Maurizio stroked her cheek. "Tesoro. Calm down."

She looked at him with squinting eyes and pursed lips. "I am calm, but they need to control themselves."

Dario made a rolling motion with his hand. "We are very sorry about this. If I knew that our presence here today would upset your father, I wouldn't have come. So sorry."

Valeria's heart warmed. "It's okay. He doesn't need to know."

Dario's hand rested at his side, but very briefly he reached across and stroked Valeria's hand, which lay on her lap. Valeria could barely breathe. She wanted to put her arms around him, to feel his warmth against hers. He made her feel things she'd never felt before and it was hard to control. Was this what it was like to be in love?

Yet she barely knew him, so how could this be love? She was being crazy, but her mind was all scattered and she couldn't think straight. His hand felt warm against her skin and when she looked over at him, his face was red and he turned away as if embarrassed. Oh, he was as shy as she was, but what would it be like to have him hold her, kiss her even?

Of course, it was forbidden. When it came to her father, everything was forbidden.

Before they left, as Ciro and Alessandra walked ahead and Carla and Maurizio hovered close behind,

Dario and Valeria spoke about her work on the farm and how she enjoyed dressmaking.

He smiled down at her. "My mama is looking for someone to make her a dress for an outing. Would you be interested in making it for her?"

Valeria was tongue-tied. "I—I don't know."

Carla intervened. "Of course she can't. Then papa will know about you being here. It's out of the question."

Dario's eyes darkened and he lowered his head.

Ciro put up his hand. "I think if we let your Papa know that Alessandra needs help with the dress then it might work. After all, Alessandra does sewing. What do you think?"

"Then why not let Alessandra sew the dress?" Maurizio asked.

Ciro shrugged and turned to his friend who said, "We'll just say that she's too busy with other clothes and would like some help."

Carla rested her hand under her chin, pondering. She turned to Valeria. "It might work you know. After all, you've wanted to get back into sewing and I'm sure I can do your share of work on the farm while you're making the dress. What do you think, Valeria?"

She felt another tingle in her stomach. "I'd love to."

Dario rubbed his hands together and smiled. "Fantastic. I'll talk to Mama."

Valeria's feet barely touched the ground as she struggled to take her eyes off Dario. He licked his lips, and her heartbeat quickened. What a great feeling she had. Yet, would it really work out? Or would her father find a way to ruin everything?

Chapter 16

SEWING MOMENT

V aleria strolled along the concrete path on her way to Alessandra's house a week later, and smiled to herself at the thought of seeing Dario. She greeted the elderly women who sat outside their houses, knitting, sewing, or embroidering with strongly fixed gazes on those who walked past. She stepped on uneven ground and felt the frosty, tireless wind cut her cheeks. It was a distraction from her dry mouth and quivering fingers. Yet, there was also a lightness in her chest and a warmth that spread through her body. She was wondering if her jelly legs would take her the rest of the way to her friend's house, which was a short distance.

Knocking on the door with a feeling of exhilaration, she waited in anticipation. Would Dario be there already or hadn't he arrived yet? What would she say to him? She didn't want to be tongue-tied and show her nervousness, but he was a gentle person and would try to make her feel at ease.

Alessandra answered the door and pulled her inside. Her eyes were lit up. "Dario's in the kitchen," she whispered. "I think he likes you."

Valeria's stomach tingled. "What?"

Alessandra edged close to her ear and whispered, "Ciro told me that Dario likes you. Besides, I could tell by the way he was looking at you the other day, girl. Take advantage of this."

Valeria's chest drummed, as she wandered in silence on the way to the kitchen. She could barely breathe, but she soldiered on. Her heart skipped a beat when her eyes met Dario's. He smiled, then turned towards his friend.

"Hey guys, look who's here," Alessandra said. She moved over to Ciro and planted a kiss on his lips.

Ciro walked towards Valeria and shook her hand. "Good to see you again. Your papa's okay with this? Making the dress for Dario's mum, I mean?"

Valeria nodded. Then Dario stepped forward and shook her hand which heated up her chest. His sweet cologne drew her closer to him.

"Nice to see you again, Valeria."

Clearing her throat and fidgeting, she whispered, "Same here."

They sat at the round table strewn with Italian magazines, a lighter, and an assortment of reference and fiction books. The kitchen sink was filled with dirty pots and pans, the benches were dirty and scratched at the edges, and the floor was covered with crumbs. The stench of cigarettes burned her nose, and she wondered whether Alessandra had tried smoking her father's cigarettes.

Ciro tapped his fingers on the table and looked at Alessandra with hungry eyes. Suddenly Dario rose and stepped out of the kitchen. Where was he going?

"What did you say to your father?" Alessandra asked.

Valeria shrugged. "Just that your friend's mother wanted me to help you make a dress."

A mischievous smile flashed across her face. "So he doesn't know about these guys?"

Valeria swallowed. "If he did, I wouldn't be here. Besides, I'm not lying. You are friends with Dario, aren't you?"

Ciro responded. "Sure, girl, but she's more my friend, if you know what I mean?" He grabbed Alessandra's hand and kissed it, a hunger burning in his eyes.

"So where's your father?" Valeria asked Alessandra.

"Oh, the usual. With his friends at the bar, enjoying his favourite pastime." A shadow filled her eyes as she turned away from Ciro and stared up at the ceiling.

Dario returned, holding a large bag of cloth and other accessories. He pushed aside the magazines and books and laid out the supplies from the bag. "This is some stuff my mama bought for you. Just some material, scissors, accessories." He unfolded a piece of paper and handed it over to Valeria, their fingers touching. "And here are her measurements so you can get started on the dress."

"Thanks," Valeria said. "It's been a while since I've sewn anything." She searched his eyes. "I appreciate you doing this for me."

Ciro leaned in and gave his friends a cheeky grin. "He had his reasons for this. "Anyway, we'll go and come back in about, say, two hours. Is that okay, Alessandra?"

"Sure. Should be enough time to at least get a start. We'll have other times to finish up." Alessandra turned back to Ciro. "We'll need to take our time on this, so that means Valera will be coming over quite often." She winked at Dario, who suddenly turned beetroot red in the face until he and Ciro rose and rushed out of the kitchen.

Dario turned back and licked his lips, staring hungrily at Valeria. "I'll see you soon." Was that a slight wink she noticed?

As soon as the boys had left, Alessandra shoved her on the shoulder. "Boy, does he have it hot for you. He couldn't take his eyes off you."

Valeria's face felt flushed. "That's ridiculous."

"Is it?" Alessandra slapped her on the shoulder again, then made room on the table by repositioning the magazines and books.

Sighing, Valeria drew a hand through her hair. "As if I could get involved with Dario. Papa would kill me. Don't you remember when—"

Alessandra's face turned pale.

How stupid could Valeria be? "I'm sorry. That wasn't your fault, not at all." She stroked her friend's shoulder and gave her a reassuring smile.

Alessandra got her colour back. "It's okay, but we'll somehow make it work. You can come here as often as you need to for the dress and Dario will keep you company. Your papa doesn't need to know. Trust me, it'll work."

"I hope you're right." Valeria had an uneasy feeling, pondering whether to take the risk. She had to be constantly on her guard when it came to her father. Would she succeed?

Valeria peered at the measurements, then cut around the outline of a dress that Dario's mother had provided to use as a model. She cut the folded material with a shaky hand, Dario's face clear in her mind. He was like a god, perfect in every way, and she wanted to see more of him. She smiled at the idea. If only her father would allow her to have a boyfriend. Maybe if he became friends with Dario's father, he'd be able to trust Dario then. Wasn't that how it was with Carla?

Shaking her head clear of Dario, Valeria pinned the front edges of the dress to the back part, and almost pricked herself with the colour-headed pins.

Alessandra started cutting out the sleeve part of the dress while whistling out a tune.

"It's great working with you," Alessandra said. "If only we could always work together."

Valeria looked up from the fabric. "That would be nice." Her heart warmed at being able to do something she loved, away from the farm. She was lucky that her father had allowed it, but maybe it would come at a price. "Maybe one day we'll work together more."

After pinning the two pieces of fabric together, they worked with the front and back part of the sleeves. She was jolted by the sound of the door slamming, and Valeria suddenly realised how quickly the time had passed. Was it two hours already? They didn't need to finish the dress today, but they'd made a good start.

Chapter 17

STOLEN KISS

Valeria turned at Ciro's voice. "We're back, so time to stop for today." He pulled Alessandra away from the table and kissed her, his hands squeezing her lower back. "Come on, let's go," he said.

Alessandra nodded. "Listen, Valeria. Ciro and I will be in my room. You don't mind keeping Dario company?" She gave her a cheeky smile.

Valeria felt giddy, her face red-hot. "That's fine."

When they left, Dario stood cross-armed, his posture stiff and his cheeks flushing. Valeria busied herself collecting and folding the pieces of fabric, then placed them in the bag. Her hands felt weak, and she couldn't stop shaking. What was wrong with her?

After a few minutes, he said, "Can I help you with that?"

She looked up with a smile. "Sure. You can put some of those loose pins back in the box. Thanks."

Dario moved in and grabbed some floating pins from the table, his eyes turning towards Valeria. The softness of his cologne penetrated the air, and her breath quickened. He stood close, and gave a nervous cough, unsure of what to say. The silence was unnerving.

Unable to hold his gaze, she turned and headed to the laundry to grab a broom.

"You're sweeping!" Dario said.

Valeria nodded. "It is a bit of mess here, don't you think?"

He shrugged. "I guess so." His eyes wandered over to the sink. "Why don't I wash up those dishes?"

"I'm sure Alessandra would appreciate that."

Dario moved over to the kitchen sink and Valeria watched his tall, lanky figure lean over the sink as he pushed up his sleeves. His forearms were tanned and taut, and she had the strongest desire to touch them.

Shaking her head, she gave the broom a forceful push and pulled her attention back to her task. Why was she having such bad thoughts about a boy?

She'd be dead if her father knew where she was. The knowledge that Alessandra was sleeping with her boyfriend without concern about her own father coming home, made things even worse.

The floor was filthy. Sweeping it all up took a while, but when she finally finished, Dario was sitting at the table reading one of the magazines.

He looked up with a smile. "Do you want to listen to some music in the living room?"

Valeria nodded. "Sure."

He headed over to the turntable and placed the needle on the vinyl record. She smiled at the hissing sound the record made before the music came on. Oh, how she loved this song with its catchy tune. *Tintarella Di Luna* by Mina was a number one hit, and it tugged at her heart with its fun-filled sound. She wanted to get up and dance.

As if he'd read her mind, Dario stood up and put out his hand. "Shall we dance?"

Valeria's cheeks warmed. "I'd like that."

He grabbed her hand and twirled her around, then held her close as if they were dancing to a slow song. His hands stroked her neck and upper back, and as he lowered his lips to her neck, she softened at his gentle touch. Valeria closed her eyes and savoured his warm kiss, feeling like her feet were floating from the ground. She never wanted his strong arms to leave her body or for the song to ever end.

Too soon, the music faded and he pulled apart from her. Approaching the record player, he took another vinyl record from the cabinet and played it on the turntable. It was a slow song with a sad, romantic tune that she didn't recognise but it instantly put her in a new mood.

Dario licked his lips as he put his arms around her and played with the strands of her hair. "You smell so nice. Are you wearing perfume?"

His voice sounded different, sexy even. "No."

As they continued to dance, he caressed her lower back, holding her tight as if never wanting to let her go. Valeria's mind was muddled and her body felt warm to his touch. She was on fire, afraid of these feelings. What if someone walked in on them dancing? What if her father suddenly showed up? If he found out she was here under false pretenses, surely she'd be dead.

This was all so wrong. She had never behaved like this before. She didn't want to feel like mush, so out of control. Yet Dario's strong, firm hands against her body made it hard to think. They only made her feel.

Dario broke away from her again as the song ended. He cupped her chin and tilted it towards him, staring hard into her eyes. Valeria stared back. She opened her mouth, waiting. His head tipped towards her, and gently, he placed his lips over hers. His tongue glided inside her mouth and a jolt shot through her at the warm wetness.

His hand slid lower down her back. Then he guided her towards the bench and eased her down, his body pressed gently over hers. His lips explored her neck, leaving a tingling heat where they touched. Then he covered her mouth with his and slid his tongue between her teeth. She gasped and arched up into him. He moaned softly as his hand found her breast and fondled it between his fingers and thumb.

Valeria thought her heart might burst from her chest. She had to stop this. It wasn't the right way to behave. She knew if she let it go on much longer, she wouldn't be able to stop herself. Quickly, she pushed him off her and sat up, smoothing her skirt.

He suddenly looked apologetic and turned away. "I'm sorry," he said. "I pushed this too far."

Valeria's body felt hot but she forced herself to ignore her desire. "I shouldn't have let it get this far."

She pressed her shirt back into place. Then her eyes roamed to the window. Luckily, no-one could see them through the grimy, white curtains.

Dario sat close beside her and took her hand. "I really like you, Valeria." He held her shoulders and turned to face him. "And I'd love to kiss you again, but not if we're rushing this."

Valeria felt a heady desire, unable to control her breathing. Just the closeness of his body made her hot for his touch, and she suddenly needed his kiss.

As if sensing her desire, Dario leaned in and brushed a strand away from her eyes, fixing his gaze before kissing her hungrily on the mouth. Valeria kissed him back and deepened the kiss, feeling dizzy with lust. What was she thinking, doing this again? She could no longer stop herself. After all, she was almost sixteen. Wasn't it normal to have these feelings between a man and a woman?

Footsteps sounded in the hall, and he pulled away. Valeria gasped as Alessandra rushed into the room, a look of concern on her face. "Hurry, you have to go. I remember my papa telling me he'd be home by four o'clock, and it's four now. I almost forgot."

Valeria hurriedly smoothed her hair, and nodded, a thickness developing in her throat. "Sure."

Dario blushed, avoiding Alessandra's gaze while Ciro smiled behind her.

"Come on, let's go, Dario," Ciro said with a smirk.

Dario looked over at Valeria, and took her hand. "I'll see you soon, Valeria." He rushed out with his friend.

"I'll be going too," Valeria said.

Alessandra shook her head. "What? No details? Is that it?"

"Papa will be worried."

Alessandra gave her a quick hug. "I'm glad you found yourself a nice guy. Enjoy it while you can."

Valeria smiled and hurriedly left the house. She still felt giddy, as if her feet couldn't touch the ground. As the door closed behind her, though, she got the sudden feeling that someone was watching her. Uneasily, she slowed her pace and glanced around. She saw no-one, but she couldn't shake the feeling of being watched. It was nothing, she told herself. Just her own overactive imagination. She couldn't help but wonder, though, if someone she knew had seen her come out of the house just after Dario had left.

Chapter 18

SHOCKING NEWS

Valeria yawned and stretched out her arms in bed, feeling warm and giddy inside. A flash of Dario's face filled her mind, and she felt goose-bumps prickle her skin. She swallowed and held the blankets over her chest, closing her eyes, and cast her mind back to the kiss and the dancing. She revisited that scene over and over, unable to think of anything else. It felt like she was in love, but was she really or was it pure lust? She hardly knew Dario, but she knew he made her feel things she'd never felt before. Was it wrong to feel this way? She wasn't old enough to get involved in such things, was she?

The snoring sounds of Elena sleeping above made her smile. If only she could share her news with Elena. But no. If she did, her sister would struggle to keep from letting something slip out to their father. It wasn't worth it.

She wanted to see Dario again, and hoped that maybe today she could help out Alessandra again. It had only been two days since she'd last seen him. Was that too soon? Would her father suspect something? She hated deceiving him, but there was no other way to have the freedom.

If she spoke to her mother about Dario, Mama would feel obligated to tell Papa. Even if she chose not to tell him, it would put strain on her mother, and she didn't want that.

Yet, as hard as it was to deceive both of them, she couldn't stop seeing Dario. He made her laugh. He was smart and handsome, and respected her. He'd stopped touching her when she put a stop to their foreplay. He was a gentleman and this made her like him even more.

Lifting off the blankets, she saw Elena sleeping. Quietly, Valeria made her way to the bathroom, feeling the coldness of the floor on her bare feet.

As she undressed and bathed, she remembered that feeling of being watched.

What if someone had seen her with Dario and relayed that little detail to her father? She'd be dead on the spot. No doubt about that. Yet why couldn't she have a boyfriend? It wasn't like she didn't have feelings. She couldn't shut them off just because her father wanted her to. She shook her head and focused on the moment. What was done was done.

Valeria rose from the bath and brushed her hair, struggling with the knots. Her hair was still too wet, and as water dripped onto the floor, she grabbed a towel to wrap around her hair. Then she made her way to the kitchen where the whole family except Elena sat around the table.

Her father eyed her closely. Then he dipped his homemade bread into a bowl of milk, turning the bread over with his spoon.

"Good morning," Valeria said.

Her father nodded and her mother approached with a kiss.

"Your hair's still wet," said Emilio.

"Go dry it properly," said Carla.

"But I promised Alessandra I'd go help with the dress today, so I'm in a rush."

Her father took a bite of his food, then lifted up his head and frowned. His eyes looked at her with curiosity as he laid down his spoon. His expression was like a look of steel, and she wished he'd say what was on his mind. "But you were only over there a few days ago. Why the rush to go again?"

Valeria's chest deflated. "But Papa, this lady wants the dress as soon as possible so we need to get it done very soon."

Her mother sipped coffee, watching Papa with a questioning look in her eyes. Was she daring to speak up for her daughter?

"Enzo," Mama said. "I think it's okay to let her go today."

Her father pursed his lips, gesturing with his hands. "We need her help on the farm today, Graziella. And that's that!"

Valeria's heart sank as she thought about Dario. She wanted so desperately to see him; and her sewing! What right did Papa have to stop her from doing something she loved? Her cheeks warmed, partly in anger, partly in embarrassment. If she was honest with herself, mostly she'd miss seeing Dario.

Carla said, "But Papa, I think we can manage without Valeria for today."

Before he could respond, there was a loud knock on the door. At the same time, Elena entered the kitchen, her eyes drooping and her hair swinging in all directions. She rubbed her eyes. "Can't people be quiet so early in the morning?"

While Elena sat and poured herself a glass of milk, Mama rose to answer the door.

Valeria looked over her shoulder towards the door, where Alessandra stood outside, shaking.

Papa turned to glance at her, then lowered his gaze and turned back around to finish his breakfast. Carla and Valeria rose to approach Alessandra. Her friend looked pale with dark circles under her eyes, as though she hadn't slept the night before.

Alessandra laid a hand on the door frame. "Good morning—" she began, and suddenly broke into tears.

Graziella touched her on the shoulder as Valeria pulled her into an embrace and stroked her hair. "What's wrong?"

They pulled apart. Alessandra rubbed her eyes and pursed her lips. She squeezed her eyes shut, her breath coming in ragged gasps. "It's my friend. He's in the hospital."

Valeria frowned? Had something happened to Ciro, or was it a school friend they hadn't seen in a while?

Alessandra put her hand over her mouth as if to stifle a cry, then moved to a stool. She drew one hand shakily through her hair, then swallowed hard. Valeria's mother poured her a glass of water. She gulped it down, and stared silently into the glass as if not knowing how to start.

Valeria walked to her friend, sat beside her and leaned forward to touch her on the shoulder. "Who are you talking about? Alessandra, who is hurt?"

Alessandra fixed her eyes strongly on Valeria, furrowing her brows. A tear fell down her cheek as she fidgeted and shifted in her seat. Looking over at her papa, Alessandra seemed to be considering her words. "I'm talking about my friend, you know—Dario. He's Ciro's friend and my friend."

Valeria's hand flew to her chest. A heavy feeling started in her stomach and she suddenly felt cold. The room blurred and a tightening in her chest felt like it would break. She shook her head as if to unhear the words. Dario? In the hospital? Dario was hurt?

She wanted to run and hide. She wanted to scream and hit something. She wanted to rush out the door and run to him, but she couldn't. Past the lump in her throat, she said, "What did you say?"

Alessandra whispered, "Dario."

Valeria's shoulders drooped. She lowered her head, holding back tears as her mother walked over to Alessandra. "I'm so sorry, dear. What can we do for you?"

Valeria tamped down a flare of resentment. Her mother's kind words should have been for her. Of course, there was no way to tell her that without admitting how she felt about Dario.

Dario...his sweet mouth, his laughing eyes...she bit the inside of her cheek to keep from crying.

Alessandra turned to Carla, then to Papa. "I need Carla's boyfriend to take me to the hospital in Salerno. Would that be okay, Carla?"

Carla nodded. "Of course. I'll ask him today when I see him later."

Valeria watched her father through lowered lashes. He dabbed his lips with a linen cloth and said, "So your friend Ciro is your boyfriend, the one you've been playing around with in the street?"

Mama shot him a dark look. "Alessandra dear, why don't you stay here with Valeria today. Then maybe later, Valeria can come with you to the hospital."

Her father shook his head. "Valeria's busy on the farm today. She'll do no such thing."

Her mother moved over to her husband. "We can manage today, Enzo. Can't you see that Alessandra needs her friend's support? She should go to the hospital."

Her father rose abruptly, shaking the table and almost dropping his glass of water. Then he stormed out of the house.

Valeria watched him, thinking how selfishly he was behaving. He always thought everything revolved around him. At least her mother had stood up for her. She'd never done that before. An uneasy feeling settled in Valeria's stomach. How would Mama's assertiveness fall back on the whole family? What would Papa's revenge be? She had no doubt there would be payback, as Papa didn't like to be challenged.

She cast her mind on Dario. How badly had he been hurt? Was he conscious or were the injuries minor? A dark shadow crossed over her as she pondered her need to be close to him at his time of need.

Chapter 19

HOSPITAL VISIT

V aleria's feet felt like lead as she walked. Each footstep brought her closer to the hospital ward. Her insides felt crumbled and she gulped down shallow breaths, thinking about Dario. The smells of disinfectant and all manner of scents made her ill. Part of her wanted to turn back, not wanting to see Dario hurt and in a hospital bed. It was hard to believe that only a couple of days ago, Dario had been holding her in his arms and squeezing her tight, making her feel like a lady. What would he look like now? How had this happened? Alessandra hadn't given any details on the ride over. Her fists clenched. Dario didn't deserve this

Watching crowds pass her by, her senses frozen, she felt Alessandra nudge her. She forced herself to focus, and her friend gave her a reassuring smile. She smiled back, half-listening to the chatter of families in the waiting room, sounds of monitors, cries of babies, the scuffle of footsteps, and the strong voices of people she assumed were the staff talking to their patients.

The hospital building was old and in need of repairs, with subtle cracks in the walls and ceilings. The flooring was uneven, and the light-fittings were in need of repair. She hated the chaos and noise, not wanting to be here at all, but it wasn't like she had a choice. Seeing Dario was important. He meant something to her.

She realised they had reached his room. Alessandra walked ahead and Valeria followed behind, staring at the floor rather than at the person lying in the bed. After Alessandra leaned over and kissed Dario on the cheek, she moved aside and ushered for Valeria to do the same. She drew back at the figure before her, but tried to contain her feelings. What she saw was shocking. Dario was bruised around both eyes, his cheeks were red and swollen, his neck had a deep cut, and there was deep discolouration and bruising around his upper chest. This was no accident. Dario had been beaten.

He gave Valeria a forced smile and sighed as he lifted himself up slightly, moaning as if he was in a lot of pain.

Valeria bent to kiss him on the cheek, but he turned his cheek and met her lips instead. She felt a slight flutter in her chest.

Alessandra stood back and crossed her arms. "So how are you feeling?"

He shrugged. "I'm alive, I guess."

Alessandra shook her head and gave him a warning look. "Don't say that."

Dario laughed slightly then turned to Valeria. "I missed you."

Valeria felt something in her stomach. She cleared her throat, eyes burning, and played with the ends of her hair. Then she took in a breath and drew closer. Alessandra started to walk out.

"What are you doing?" Valeria asked.

"I'm giving you guys some privacy, but I'll be back soon."

They watched her leave. Then Dario moved forward and grabbed Valeria's hand. He pulled her towards him, so Valeria obliged. He kissed her lightly on the mouth, and Valeria felt weak in the knees.

What was he doing in this state? She pulled back and shook her head.

"How can you be kissing me at a time like this?"

He beamed. "But I missed you, particularly those lips."

She managed a brief smile. "Who did this to you?"

Dario turned away. He looked over at the man beside him, who was sleeping. He put his hand over his mouth as if thinking, then looked back at her. "It was just an accident."

"What kind of accident?"

"The normal kind."

Valeria grabbed his hand, stroking it. "Please tell me who beat you up. I need to know."

His eyes darkened. "You don't need to know anything. I'm fine."

Valeria lowered her head, wondering what to say next. The more she looked at him, the more certain she was. She could see he'd been beaten up badly. This was no car or bike accident. A human being had hit him with rage. Even the deep cut must've been traumatic for Dario, but he wasn't about to tell her anything. It was if he was trying to hide what he felt. Was he trying to be strong for her, so she'd worry less?

She leaned in closer. "Someone was obviously angry with you. Why, Dario?"

Dario licked his lips. "Can you get me the water over there, please?"

Valeria shook her head. "Don't change the subject."

He fidgeted, averting his eyes. "I need water."

Valeria picked up the glass and handed it to him, but he spilled some of it on his chest. "Do you need help?"

He turned away again with a clenched fist and reddening cheeks. "I'm not an invalid. I can manage just fine."

"I'm sorry. I didn't mean to—"

His breathing became heavy. "Forget it!"

The next few minutes went by in silence as Valeria chose to sit on a chair waiting for Dario to speak. The air was thick with tension and Dario sipped his drink and seemed to shudder with each movement.

She wondered if he was in some kind of trouble with the wrong kind of people. Was it about drugs? Yet, he didn't seem the type to intentionally cause trouble. He had a big heart, and seemed to want to help people rather than make trouble for others.

Alessandra finally returned and Valeria was relieved. The silence was killing her. It was obvious that Dario didn't like her prying, but what did he expect? He'd been beaten to a pulp.

Alessandra sat on the edge of the bed. "So where's Ciro?"

His eyes were dark, his posture slouched. "He left a while before you came. How did you get here?"

"Carla and Maurizio dropped us off. They're waiting for us back in the foyer area," Alessandra said. "So how did this happen? Get into one of your fights with Ciro?"

He chuckled. "I wish that was it."

Alessandra looked to Valeria with a frown. "Tell us who did this."

"Oh, not you too. I had an earful from Valeria, and I'm tired of it. Just let it go."

Valeria rose out of her chair and approached him. She looked down at him then kissed him on the forehead. "Are you involved in drugs?"

Dario lifted his eyebrows, then laughed. "Are you crazy?"

"Then what is it? What's going on with you?"

Dario looked down the line of his bed, fixing his gaze away from both of them. He sucked in a breath and said, "This is something I can never tell either of you, so you might as well leave."

Valeria and Alessandra simply stared at each other, dumbfounded.

Chapter 20

NEW DISCOVERY

After leaving the hospital, Valeria sat in the car with her head bowed, a sick feeling in her stomach. She watched through the window to distract herself from dark thoughts. Outside, in a whirl, cows grazed, a flock of birds soared, and burly men in hardhats and overalls dug drainage trenches by the side of the road. Eventually her stomach settled as she watched the mountainous background behind the old buildings and the Cathedral, all distracting her from Dario's accident.

Pulling her mind back to the image of Dario's fragile state, her leg muscles felt tight and a wave of heat flooded her body. As she fidgeted constantly in her seat, Alessandra grabbed her hand and smiled.

"Don't worry. We'll get to the bottom of this. We'll speak to Ciro. He'll know what's going on."

Carla turned back from the front seat, frowning. "So what do you think happened to Dario?"

Alessandra drew a hand through her hair. "He wouldn't tell us, but he looked concerned about something." She scratched her temple. "If you ask me, he might be in some kind of trouble."

Valeria found her voice. "What kind of trouble?"

Alessandra shrugged. "Some kind of thug, I guess. I don't think it's the Mafia, but someone obviously hates him. That, or it's some kind of warning."

Valeria's shoulders drooped. She clutched her stomach as if it would burst. A painful tightness in her throat stopped her from crying as she shut out those around her. Unable to meet their gazes, she stared out the window as if in a deep trance.

She sensed something about the way Dario had kissed her; a sense of longing or an air of desperation. It was almost as if he couldn't get enough of her, but why would he feel that way? She was there for him. Did he think she wouldn't be? Or was he planning on letting her go for some reason?

Alessandra's sudden announcement of their arrival jolted Valeria from her seat. Valeria glanced out the window and realised they were in Laurino. She hadn't even noticed.

"Can you stop by Ciro's house, Maurizio?" Alessandra asked. "I need to talk to him."

Carla answered for him. "You go alone! Valeria's coming straight home. Papa will have a fit if she's not back with me."

Alessandra sighed. "Can't you just wait for us? I won't be long. We'll only be five minutes."

Carla turned back around and pursed her lips. "You will go there alone and we'll wait for you in the car."

"You don't give up, do you?" Alessandra said.

"Well, if you don't want to see Valeria's funeral, you'd better get out quick."

Maurizio eventually stopped in front of a dilapidated house. Alessandra zoomed out before the car had stopped rolling, and knocked on the door. With a heavy heart, Valeria watched a stout man open the door. He smiled at Alessandra, giving her a quick peck on the cheek, then opened the door wide to let her in.

Valeria waited in the car with bated breath. Carla and Maurizio chattered amongst themselves, and Valeria was fine with that. They must've realised she wasn't in a talking mood so left her alone. She watched passers-by carrying shopping bags, a mother holding her daughter's hand, and a group of boys laughing and being rowdy. What if that was the group that had hurt Dario? What if they were the ones who beat him badly enough to send him to the hospital?

Oh, now she was really losing it. Making up imaginary stories based on people who passed her by. This was madness. She was going crazy, and didn't know how to stop her rushing thoughts. The wait for Alessandra was too long, and her whole body ached from the length of time she'd sat in the car.

She leaned forward and said over the front seat, "I just need a stretch. Is that okay?"

Carla turned and nodded, so Valeria opened the car door and felt a rush of cold wind brush her face. The sounds of people walking by kept her grounded as she watched the door at Ciro's house, waiting and hoping that Alessandra would finally come out.

If only she could go in. She might learn something about Dario, but she knew Carla wouldn't let her. She'd have to keep waiting.

She rolled her shoulders and walked around the car a bit to stretch her muscles, then turned to get into the back seat. Alessandra finally hurried out of the house and headed to the car. Her face looked white and her expression was grim.

Valeria swallowed. "I knew it! He's involved in the Mafia, isn't he?"

Alessandra gave a nervous laugh. "I'm not really sure."

Valeria's feet felt frozen. "What do you mean you're not sure?"

Alessandra turned away as if contemplating. She bit her lip and briefly closed her eyes. "Dario and Ciro witnessed something, and it got them into trouble."

Valeria suddenly felt cold and shivered. "What did they witness?"

Alessandra looked away. "That's all Ciro told me. He said that they were threatened not to tell anyone about the details or they'd be in even bigger trouble." She exhaled. "Ciro was hurt too, but not as badly as Dario." Her eyes dampened. "I felt this coldness from Ciro. It was like he didn't want anything to do with me. He pushed me away and acted like I was dirt. He wouldn't even kiss me goodbye. He was aloof and couldn't even look me in the eye. I don't know, Valeria. They're both in some kind of trouble, and it scares me."

Valeria swayed on her feet, suddenly light-headed. Alessandra grabbed her by the arm to steady her.

Whatever Dario had seen must have been serious. Maybe it was Mafia-related after all.

Chapter 21

RECOVERY

Valeria sat hunched on a stool in her kitchen. With shaky fingers, she was sewing the hem of Dario's mother's dress in a trance-like state. Nothing looked real to her. It was as if she was walking in a fog, a density in the air that stopped her from seeing her way forward. She was dimly aware of her sisters' voices in the next room. It felt strange to be working on the dress in her own home, but with Dario in the hospital, there was no need for her to work exclusively at Alessandra's house.

It had been a few days since Alessandra had given her the news about Dario. Nothing made sense anymore. She'd worried about what might happen if her father found out about her relationship with Dario. It had never occurred to her that Dario might wind up with even bigger troubles of his own. She wanted to be by his side, but instead he was pushing her away.

Thinking about the danger Dario was in, Valeria felt sick. Whoever had beaten him up wanted him to keep quiet about something, but what? What had Dario witnessed? A feeling of unease settled in her stomach as she blinked back tears. It was a hopeless situation.

The prick of the needle against her forefinger jerked her back to the present, and instinctively she brought the bleeding finger to her mouth. Wincing, she glanced at the dress and noted with relief that none of the blood had dripped onto the cloth. Then she rose and headed to the bathroom, pressing hard on her finger to stop the bleeding. The chilling water eased the sting, and she held her finger under the tap until the bleeding stopped and the throbbing had subsided.

From the front of the house, Carla's voice, then Alessandra's, caught her attention. Hurriedly, she dried her finger with a towel and rushed to the front door where Carla stood eyeing Alessandra. Valeria resisted the urge to hug her friend, who looked like she was about to cry.

"Are you okay, Alessandra?" Carla asked.

She nodded dully and turned to Valeria. "I need to speak to you."

Valeria took her friend's hand and together they sat on the bench in silence for a few minutes. With a speculative glance over her shoulder, Carla left them and sauntered to her bedroom.

"What is it?" Valeria asked.

Tears rolled down Alessandra's face. "Ciro and I broke up."

Valeria reached for her friend's hand. "I'm so sorry. What happened?"

She shrugged. "I don't know. That's the mystery."

Valeria cleared her throat. "Well, what happened, exactly?"

Alessandra's shoulders drooped. She looked up to the ceiling as if the answer was etched onto it. Then she turned back to Valeria. "Yesterday, he just said that we don't work, and that we—we don't have a future together." She bowed her head and choked back a sob. Valeria patted her on the shoulder and waited for more. After rubbing her eyes, Alessandra went on. "He said—said that he doesn't have feelings for me anymore. That it's over, just like that."

Valeria found the suddenness of the breakup strange. Something must've happened to make him feel that way. He'd always doted on Alessandra and obviously cared for her. How could that change so suddenly?

"There must be some explanation for this, Alessandra. Ciro cares about you."

Alessandra shrugged. "I don't know. That's all he said." Her gaze fixed on Valeria's. "I even asked him about Dario a few times, but he said nothing. I think he knows but just didn't want to tell me."

"It's okay. Don't worry about that. I'm more worried about you."

Alessandra swallowed, then gave a bitter laugh. "You know what? I'm better off without that jerk anyway. He wasn't really my type."

Valeria sighed. "Don't even joke about this."

Alessandra wiped the tears from her cheeks with her palms. "I'm not joking. Besides, he was too young for me. He's not man enough for me."

Valeria shook her head, realising what her friend was doing. Trying to make herself feel better. She'd go with it for now. Let Alessandra heal in her own time.

"I'm here for you, Alessandra. Whenever you need to talk, I'm your support. Always."

Alessandra nodded. "Thanks, but I'll be fine. I can find myself a new man. I don't need Ciro."

Valeria had a bad feeling. "Just give yourself time to heal. Don't jump into anything."

"Why not? I'm free to do as I like now."

Valeria shook her head. "Alessandra, please. Just take your time."

Alessandra's gaze turned inward, and a sly smile spread across her lips. "I'm free to see Gregorio now. He's a real man."

Valeria's breath quickened. She couldn't believe what she was hearing. Of all people, Alessandra had to pick Gregorio. She couldn't help but feel like her friend was making a huge mistake.

Chapter 22

GRIM NEWS

A few days later, Valeria sat at Alessandra's kitchen table, finishing the embroidery on the dress she'd made for Dario's mother. She had only this last rose to complete, and Dario should be here any moment to pick up the dress. It had been just over a week since the incident and Dario would be in a position to travel by now. She might get answers about his attack.

Shifting her weight to relieve the hardness of the stool, she added the finishing touches to the dress, then placed it in a bag. She stretched and yawned as fatigue settled in from lack of sleep and stress over everything that had happened. She'd tossed and turned for days, worrying about both Alessandra and Dario.

Right now, her friend was having a hard discussion with her father, who was drunk again. Hearing the door slam, Valeria assumed he must've left for the nearest bar with his drinking buddies. She could only imagine how badly her friend must feel, but Alessandra never said how it affected her. She never complained, putting up with her father's actions because he gave her the freedom she believed she craved but didn't really want. Valeria had come to realise that what Alessandra really wanted was security but since her father never gave her that, she coped any way she could to survive. Her friend never really got it. Hopefully, Alessandra would understand in her own time.

Valeria heard footsteps as Alessandra rushed into the kitchen. "Dario's here. Are you ready to see him?"

Valeria's heart quickened. Her thoughts had been so scattered, she had failed to hear he was at the door. Her feet seemed frozen on the spot and her throat had dried up like a prune. It was now or never.

"Call him in. I'll wait here."

Alessandra nodded, then turned to leave, calling over her shoulder, "I'll be in my room if you need me."

A few seconds later, Dario came in and forced a smile. His eyes looked dull and his posture slumped. He leaned in towards Valeria and laid his hands on her shoulders. With a penetrating gaze, he inched his face closer to hers and kissed her deeply on the mouth. She returned the kiss, enjoying the warmth of his mouth. Then the kiss grew deeper and hungrier, their tongues dancing and their arms holding each other tight. He held her desperately, as if not wanting to let her go. The urgency in his kiss unsettled her.

Dario pulled back, then gestured for her to join him at the kitchen table, his head lowered.

"I have some bad news, Valeria."

A needle of pain pricked her heart. "Before you say anything, I know why you were beaten up."

Dario's head jerked up, his face turning crimson. "What are you talking about?"

Easy, Valeria! Just breathe! "I know you witnessed something and got in trouble."

His shoulders slumped, but he didn't deny it. Instead, he seemed suddenly distant, his mind a million miles away.

"Is that true?" she pressed.

He came back to the present. "Who told you?"

"Alessandra."

"Damn Ciro."

Valeria turned her head from side to side. "You need to tell me the truth, Dario. What happened?"

He lowered his head again, as if to hide the tears that glistened in his eyes. "No, Valeria. That's where you're wrong. I don't need to tell you anything. This will never work out. You and I cannot be together."

Valeria felt a stabbing pain settle in the centre of her chest. She swallowed hard, refusing to cry. She wouldn't give in to that weakness.

"I want to help," she said. "Just tell me what happened, and then we can decide what to do."

He held his hand up. "I—it's not going to work. I can't be with you and that's that. I'm sorry, Valeria." He pressed his shaking hands to his thighs and turned away.

Valeria forced a calmness she didn't feel into her voice. "But why? Don't you care about me?"

Dario looked away, hesitating. "I'm not ready to settle down. I'm too young and plan to see other girls. You're just not right for me."

Valeria forced her words past the tightness in her chest and throat.

"You could've told me that before. Why string me along?"

He looked down again, his hands fidgeting. "I'm sorry."

"Can you at least tell me who beat you up?"

He fixed his gaze on her eyes. "I can't tell you that, Valeria." He reached for her hand but she pulled it away.

Valeria rose. "Well, have a nice life! Good luck to you!"

Dario sat transfixed until she crossed her arms and glared at him. He eventually rose too, slowly, clumsily, as if in a daze then stalled as if not wanting to leave. He shuffled his feet and stared into her eyes as if he wanted to drink her.

She shook her head. "Just leave." Valeria then put up her hand. "Wait! Take your mother's dress." She placed it in a plastic bag.

Dario nodded, picked up the bag then shambled out of the house. He didn't turn back.

Valeria sank to the floor and put her hands over her face, feeling the coolness of her palms against her wet cheeks. It was over before it even began, and now she'd never see Dario again. She already ached for the taste of his mouth.

The sound of a bang at the front door made her stomach leap. Had Dario returned to tell her he was changing his mind? That he wanted to be with her after all? Maybe they had a chance to be together and they could work it out. A glimmer of hope surged.

Rising from the floor, she headed to the door. Alessandra was three steps ahead and swung the door open. It wasn't Dario after all. It was Gregorio.

Chapter 23

REBOUND

Valeria pulled back and watched from the kitchen, careful to be quiet as Gregorio swaggered into the house. He pinned Alessandra to the wall and held her arms over her head. Then he kissed her on the mouth. His hands moved down to her breasts, squeezing them one by one. He kissed her breasts, then he lifted up her dress and started touching her.

Alessandra moaned, then shot a glance at Valeria and squirmed away. "Let's go to my room."

He smiled, patted her on the bottom, and headed to her room. Valeria wanted to scream out to her friend that she was making a huge mistake. How could she convince Alessandra that she was simply missing Ciro and settling for the next best thing?

After a few minutes, she crept to Alessandra's bedroom. Maybe she could stop this from happening. Then she thumped a fist into her palm. Who was she kidding? Alessandra wouldn't listen to her when she was in the throes of grief over losing Ciro. Hearing the bed creak, the banging on the wall, and the moans from her friend, Valeria felt sick to her stomach. Gregorio screamed out, "Oh yeah, baby, right there!"

Valeria stood frozen to the floor, shaking her head. She needed to get out of there. Her breath quickening, she ran out of the house and into the streets, trying to ignore the people passing by and those sitting on rickety chairs. Her mind was in a haze and all she could think of was Gregorio touching Alessandra and screaming out about his pleasure. How could he have sex with a fifteen-year-old? Didn't he have any morals? What would his mother think? Valeria knew without a doubt that Giovanna wouldn't approve of this relationship, if you could call it that. She wanted to cry and pull her hair out. If only Alessandra would take the time to grieve for Ciro, as Valeria would for Dario.

Her feet and legs ached, and her shoulders tensed. She slowed from a run to a walk and passed by the houses, not greeting any of the women with their prying eyes. She'd probably get a scolding by her parents, telling her she was impolite and should've greeted the onlookers, but all she wanted was to get home and crawl into bed. She wished she could forget the whole incident, but she knew she couldn't. Somehow she had to convince Alessandra to stay away from that man.

A quiet snore brought her back to the present. Giovanna was dozing in a chair in front of her own house, a few metres away from Valeria's house. Mind reeling, Valeria realised she was almost home and broke into a trot. Her toe caught on a raised bit of concrete and she fell forward, crashing headlong into Giovanna. As if in slow motion, the chair toppled backwards. Momentum carried Valeria forward, and she gasped at the crushing pain of her chest against the older woman's, the knock of her ankle against the leg of the chair and the split skin over her hands. Giovanna hit the ground with a grunt and a screech as her head struck a potted plant with a sickening thud.

"Oh no, my head!" Giovanna clutched it as she tried to lift herself up. Blood trickled from between her fingers. "Stupid girl! Get off me!" She pushed Valeria off, groaning while Valeria lifted herself up and turned around to see many eyes watching the scene.

Valeria felt the sting of her grazed and bloody hands, the bruising on her chest, and the sprain of her ankle. She soon felt two arms grab her from behind, and when she turned, she was looking into her mother's eyes.

"Valeria, are you okay, dear?"

Then her throat closed as her father rushed over and said, "What have you done now, Valeria?" He bent down and righted the chair, with Giovanna still in it. When the woman had calmed down, he put one arm around her and walked her to their house.

Valeria hobbled along behind while Giovanna put all her weight on Papa. He glared at Valeria over his shoulder and shook his head as if she'd done it on purpose.

Her body felt too heavy for her legs as she forced one step in front of the other. Her mother slid under her right arm and supported Valeria with her own strength. As they neared the house, her brother and sisters opened the door, wide-eyed. Carla pointed a finger at Valeria and raised a questioning brow as she realised that Giovanna was hurt. Valeria's throat tightened. She hadn't meant to knock into that woman, but she had. Now it was time to fix her up and take her back home.

Giovanna lay on the bench while Valeria sat on a stool. Her mother fetched a bucket with warm water, dipped a cloth into it, then dabbed on Giovanna's head wound, which was streaming with blood. Carla tended to Valeria by bandaging her ankle and washing her hands with warm water. Her father had left as soon he came inside. Typical of him to not pull his weight. Typical of him not to care.

Giovanna had her eyes closed as she lay down. Her lips squeezed together as if she was in pain. "Your daughter needs to learn some manners."

Her mother turned to her. "Valeria, please apologise."

Valeria's ankle was throbbing. "I'm sorry. I honestly didn't mean to hurt you. I just tripped."

Giovanna grunted. "Too busy thinking about nothing, that's what it was. No respect for the elderly anymore."

Carla gave Valeria a reassuring smile. "It was an accident, Giovanna. Valeria did apologise, and your head will heal nicely and quickly."

Giovanna grunted again in response.

Valeria felt a flash of anger. A wash of guilt followed the anger. She didn't like the old woman, but she hadn't meant to hurt her.

Sometime later, her father stepped into the house with the doctor behind him.

"The doctor here has kindly offered to visit but we had to wait for his other patients. Now let him look at both of you." He turned to the man. "Nothing too serious, doctor."

The doctor approached and checked Giovanna first. Valeria's ankle throbbed, but she waited in silence, hoping her neighbour's injuries weren't severe. She frowned when Giovanna pressed her shaky hands against her temple. She must be in a lot of pain, Valeria thought and lowered her head.

What a terrible day this had been—and with Dario gone and Alessandra sleeping with Gregorio, it didn't look like things were going to get better.

Chapter 24

THE NEW SLAVE

Valeria trudged down the dirt path from the farm towards Giovanna's house. Her ankle had healed, and now she was headed to meet her fate. Her father's words rang in her head. "You are going to run errands for Giovanna as punishment for hurting her. For at least a week, maybe even two."

"But Papa! It wasn't my fault."

"You'll do as I say and that's that." The flint in his eyes told her there would be no reprieve.

Now, with slouched shoulders and a heavy heart, she watched the ground and sighed, hugging her body to brave the cold, misty air. She couldn't believe her father was forcing her to be Giovanna's servant. Why did he have to be so mean? It wasn't like she did it on purpose, and it wasn't like he was perfect by any means. It wasn't fair she had to suffer with that toxic woman who wouldn't even accept her apology.

Panting for breath after an hour-long walk, she pressed her arms into her sides and smelled freshly baked pastries as she passed the pasticceria. Normally, the sweet, buttery smell would lift her spirits, but not today. She spotted women chasing children down the street on uneven ground, the children kicking down pebbles and loose stones in her path. Valeria gnawed at her cheek, wanting to scream at those children. You'd think they had nothing better to do. What right did they have to cause such havoc on the street?

A wry smile crept across her face as she realised maybe she was just angry with her situation, not the children.

She wished she was back at the farm, even though Gregorio was working on the cowshed. She'd managed to ignore his presence and help her mother prepare pickled vegetables then store them in clay jars. The day had been productive until she had to leave for her forced servitude. Her chest felt tight and her hands felt numb in the cooler spring air.

Stepping in front of Giovanna's door, she took a deep breath and knocked. The wait seemed to take forever, and Valeria was almost about to leave when

Giovanna finally opened the door and said with a grimace, "About time. Aren't you late?"

Valeria shrugged. "I'm coming from the farm. It's not close."

Giovanna shook her head, then opened the door wider to let her in.

The house felt colder than it was outside but everything lay in its place. Rusty pots and pans hung over the kitchen, wooden stools stood around the kitchen bench, an iron stood perched on a table in the corner, and assorted shoes were stacked neatly in a shoe rack against the back wall.

Valeria stood awkwardly while Giovanna ushered her over to the kitchen and started pushing out a sack of flour from a spare room. The old woman grabbed a bowl, and said, "Well—don't—just stand there. Help me carry the flour over here." She wiped her sweating brow, holding the edge of the counter for support.

Valeria rushed to the sack of flour, pulled it over towards the bench, and then placed the bowl into the sack, a whole heap falling onto her pants. Giovanna blew out an impatient breath and pushed her aside. "Let me do that." She poured out the flour-filled bowl and emptied it into an even larger bowl, then scooped the smaller bowl back into the sack of flour. She poured it into the bigger bowl sitting on the bench.

Valeria wasn't sure why she was needed if Giovanna could cook on her own. She might've needed help carrying heavy things but that was it. All she seemed to want to do was boss Valeria around. Well, she didn't need to be told what to do when her mother had taught her perfectly well. Her dry throat wanted to speak but then it'd get back to her father. She didn't need further punishment. Coming here and being ordered around was humiliating enough.

She turned to Giovanna who took out a discoloured creased piece of paper with squiggly writing. Valeria could hardly make out the words.

Giovanna handed the note to Valeria. "Here! You make the bread from this recipe and I'll rest my feet. I'm feeling tired today."

"But Mama taught me how to make bread. I don't need the recipe."

Giovanna glared. "You better not speak back to me or I'll let your papa know. He'll dish out more punishment for you. Now, follow this recipe because it's my way of making bread and not your mama's way."

Valeria swallowed, a hard ball forming in her chest. She clenched her fists, watched Giovanna saunter down the corridor to her room, and lowered her head at the bowls of flour. She wanted to go home. Giovanna was more than capable.

Since she was stuck with the bread-making, she followed the recipe and kneaded the dough while pouring flour over her fingers to remove the stickiness. Pressing hard into the dough, she punched it until it was stiff, then set it on a flat timber board, sprinkling more flour. She shaped the dough into six loaves and let them rest and rise for a couple of hours.

She washed her hands, picking at the sticky dough and feeling the warm water soothe her dry skin. She wished again for some cream, something to make her hands soft, like a rich girl with no need to do hard labour.

After wiping the benches, she sighed and shifted her weight. Her legs ached from standing so long. She tiptoed to the door of the other room and listened. Sounds of snoring came from inside. She suppressed a giggle. What a snore coming from Giovanna. She could easily wake up the dead. Relieved, Valeria slid onto the bench for a short rest, then put her feet up and closed her eyes.

She wondered how long she had to stay here. She assumed she had to be home by dinner. She'd done her duty and made the homemade bread. Would she get to take some home or was it all for Giovanna and Gregorio?

She'd almost dozed off when the door squeaked open. Quickly, she rose and took a deep breath. It was Gregorio and her father coming in the door. Papa's glare suddenly said it all, and she fidgeted with her hands and forced a smile.

Chapter 25

THE MYSTERY

Valeria stiffened as she rose. "Papa! What are you doing here?"

He stormed into the house and gestured with his hands, shaking his head. "What do you think I'm doing here?"

"Can I come home now?" He grunted in response. "Papa, please."

He turned his head from side to side. Gregorio fixed his gaze on Valeria. "Why are you lying down when your job is to help Giovanna around the house? What is that? Laziness? Are you not learning your lesson here after what you did to Giovanna?"

"But Papa, the bread is cooking in the oven and I didn't know what else to do. Giovanna is resting in her room."

He ignored her response and pulled her by the hair, then shoved her into the kitchen. "I want you to sweep or find something else to do. I will wait here until you're done." He headed over to the bench and sat.

Valeria held back tears, her scalp aching from the hard pull of her hair. It was like he wasn't listening, or refused to listen. It was always his way or no way so she never won.

When she finished sweeping the kitchen, she went back into the living room. Her father sat on the bench with Gregorio, who looked up and said, "My mama would probably like you to clean out those shelves." He pointed to a shelf filled with chipped plates, small rusty pots, and ceramic bowls that were not in their proper place. She nodded sullenly and took them out one by one, arranging them so that each item was grouped together.

Gregorio rose as she was finishing. "I will check on Mama."

"Okay," Valeria said. Yet what did she care if he did that? She wasn't his keeper.

Her father had fallen asleep on the bench. Quietly, she put the broom back in the closet. She crossed her arms, not knowing what to do next. Should she wake her father so they could go home or should she wait for Gregorio to return from the room?

Time crept on and Gregorio hadn't returned. Out of curiosity, she tiptoed down the corridor and glanced into the rooms. In one of them, Giovanna was snoring the tiles off the roof. It was laughable that she'd slept this long while Valeria did her dirty work. The coldness of the corridor led her to another room. She peered into the room where Gregorio was hunched over, his back towards her. What was he doing?

She took slow deep breaths, trying hard not to make noise. Gregorio was putting something into a drawer. She couldn't see what it was until he dropped something on the floor. It was a stack of liras. Was that what he was counting? Money! It looked like a lot of money. He grabbed a key from his pocket then locked the drawer.

Valeria knew he couldn't get paid that much doing the cowshed. Her father couldn't afford that kind of wage. Maybe he had another job. She might've remembered her mother telling her he did maintenance work for the village but that wouldn't have paid much.

She was lost in her thoughts until someone tapped her on the shoulder.

"What are you doing here, Valeria?"

She turned to her father, then heard Gregorio's footsteps nearing. She looked up and saw that Gregorio's face was bright red.

"Mr Allegro, I didn't know Valeria was there. I just came here to put some things away."

Her father frowned, his lips pursed. "Valeria? I asked you a question."

She shrugged. "Nothing. I was just checking on Giovanna. Then I heard something in this room, but I didn't know it was Gregorio's room, Papa. I didn't know."

His hands were on his hips. "You should've left straight away and not be spying on him. It's his business what he does in his room. Now, let's go. You'll be back here tomorrow afternoon and the next afternoon after that. In fact, for one whole week you will be here until you learn to behave and have learned your lesson."

He pulled her by the arm then nodded to Gregorio, who was still blushing.

She turned to Gregorio. "The bread is still in the oven and it will be ready soon."

His eyes darkened, and he bit on his lip, a penetrating glare plastered on his face. She suddenly felt sick.

Chapter 26

WALKING ON EGG SHELLS

On the farm, Graziella heaved a timber crate full of pickled vegetables off a bench. It was drizzling, and she paused to wipe the rain from her face.

Not far away, Enzo and his friend laughed raucously as they hauled a squealing pig out of his pen. She frowned as Enzo slashed the throat of the pig in the drizzle. Ignoring the crimson stains on his clothes, he watched its blood dripping into a bucket as the pig drew its last breath. The crimson droplets of blood smeared over his clothes. Sickened, Graziella turned away, picking up the crate and panting with exertion as she carried the unwieldy object into the outside kitchen. Arms aching, she bent to lower it to the floor. It slipped from her grasp and landed with a thud, narrowly missing her foot. She'd never adapted to the slaughter of the pigs, even though it was necessary for their survival. Her heart constantly tugged whenever the dead eyes of the pig stared back.

As she sat on a stool, she wiped her sweaty brow and pondered a discussion she'd had with Valeria two days ago. Both she and Valeria wondered why Gregorio had come to stay with his mother. It clearly wasn't out of love or duty but something else entirely. Graziella couldn't put her finger on it, but she knew Giovanna must be useful to him in some way. There was no love lost between them, and she sensed that Gregorio would someday fight back against her taunts. He was a proud man who seemed capable, but when his mother was around, he floundered. She was afraid Giovanna would push him to his limits.

Valeria had mentioned something about liras he kept stashed in a drawer. The thought made Graziella's skin prickle. She knew Gregorio wouldn't make that much money just by helping out here and in his maintenance duties. No, the money came by other means, and she was sure it was nothing proper or even legal. There was something unsettling about

Gregorio. Something unscrupulous, yet somehow lost. How could she keep Valeria away from him? There had to be a way to convince Enzo to stop Valeria from attending to Giovanna's needs. She had to get on Enzo's good side, cautious not to anger him. She cringed at confrontation, and always had.

Moments later, footsteps jolted Graziella out of her reverie. She turned, her heart racing. Enzo handed her a wooden container. "Here, make the prosciutto, Graziella. No time for you to waste and sit there doing nothing."

She nodded. "Where are the shoulders and legs of the pig?"

"They're coming! I'll be back."

Graziella sighed. She wished he didn't have to be so abrupt with her all the time, but that was his way. She'd lived with it for many years and he wasn't about to change now. For the most part, she accepted his temperament, knowing that, beneath the hurt and anger, he was a good man who took his duty to take charge seriously.

When Enzo returned with the parts of the pig which had been hosed outside, Graziella carried the meat to the sink where it had to be rewashed for extra cleanliness. As she stood by the tap, Enzo touched her on the shoulder. "You need to talk to that daughter of yours. She's not learning her lesson."

"What—with how you mentioned her resting on the bench?"

He crossed his arms and pursed his lips. "Yes, that's not right. She was there for a purpose. To do her duty by Giovanna."

Graziella wanted to be cautious with her words and not rock the boat. "But my understanding is that she made the bread while Giovanna slept." His expression darkened, so she toned down her words. "Valeria's still going there, Enzo. She is fine with helping out."

With a shake of his head, his veins appeared to pop out his head. "She's getting too independent for my liking. She answers me back, and has an answer for everything. I don't think she's taking her duty with Giovanna seriously."

Graziella's chest tightened at the thought of Valeria's growing assertiveness. She was worried for her daughter, as Enzo was not a man you could turn against. You'd never win, but Valeria was idealistic and didn't know the ways of life yet. She'd have to learn the hard way. She'd have to respect her father as her protector, and the man who was in charge, but how could Graziella warn her daughter about that? Valeria was too strong-minded for her own good, just like Elena. Sometimes Graziella's heart seized with fear for her girls.

"I will speak to her, Enzo. She is just growing up and trying to find her feet. It's natural for a teenager to want to have fun rather than have all these duties. She is a hard worker and has not defied you." *Dare she take the chance to say more?* "Maybe once she's finished with Giovanna, she can get back to her sewing."

He grunted. "We'll see."

"Well, she enjoyed making that dress for her friend's mother."

He glared. "Like I said, we will see. You do not have to tell me twice."

She nodded, a quick apology. "And what do you think of Gregorio?"

Enzo knit his brows. "He's a solid worker. Why do you ask?"

Graziella chose her words carefully. "I don't know if I trust him completely, Enzo." Her stomach felt tight as she watched the blank expression on his face.

He huffed. "He's a man who works hard, and I trust him. So just leave it at that."

Enzo stormed off, leaving Graziella feeling flushed. Why didn't Enzo sense something strange in Gregorio? He might work hard on the farm but that didn't mean he was trustworthy. She'd just have to keep an eye on him, and make sure Valeria was safe. That was all she could do. She had no real evidence that he was doing anything shifty.

She took a deep breath as she placed the legs and shoulder pieces of the pig into the clay dish. Then adding her fingers into a jar of salt, she grabbed several handfuls and spread it over the meat. The cold stickiness of the salt stuck to her skin as she pressed it into the fatness of the meat and rough surfaces. She added more salt, rubbing it firmly into the meat, feeling some of the sprinkles on her skin burn a few cuts she had. Once finished, she washed her hands and hooked the meat to hang from the ceiling to cure. In two weeks, she would wash it again with wine, then add chilli and pepper. Then it would be left to be dry for about six months, and they would have their homemade prosciutto.

As she washed her hands, she thought again of Valeria at the house with Gregorio, and an uneasy feeling settled in her chest. She would have to be vigilant until she could convince Enzo to put an end to Valeria's punishment.

Chapter 27

ACCIDENT

V aleria strolled along the path, feeling a presence behind her. As she turned, Dario appeared in the distance. He veered in the opposite direction as if he wanted to avoid her. Was he watching her? And why was he following her? She was done with him. He had made that very clear, and she couldn't bear to see his handsome face when there was no future for them. If he had wanted her out of his life, he didn't need to linger. It only made things worse. It made her feel as if she was being stabbed.

Shaking off the thoughts, Valeria knocked on Giovanna's door and stepped inside as soon as it swung open. Giovanna grabbed her by the hand without so much as a greeting, and pulled her into the kitchen.

"Today, you're making biscuits for me. I need to step out for a few minutes."

Valeria spotted Gregorio on the bench and drew back. He lay on his back with his arms over his head, yawning. He was chewing on something, his mouth making harsh sounds that irked her. She turned away, choosing to ignore him, and focused on Giovanna. "Where are you going?"

Giovanna's eyes widened. "Well, it's really none of your business, but I have a few things to get at the shop. You just do what you're told. I have the recipe written on that note over there." She pointed to a gritty note filled with oil stains.

Valeria wanted to shake her head but found herself nodding instead. How could Giovanna think it was appropriate to leave a young woman alone here with her grown son? He made Valeria uncomfortable. Besides, what if her father found out she was alone with Gregorio? He'd eat her for breakfast.

There was no winning this. She had to fulfil her duties, even though Giovanna didn't need the help, but she was sure to be punished if her father found her alone with a man.

That flash of anger returned as Valeria stalked towards the kitchen. Who knew how long Giovanna would be gone? She would probably linger at the shop, chattering away with a friend while Valeria slaved over a hot oven on her own.

Peering at the recipe, Valeria started taking out the flour then the sugar. Gregorio rose from the bench and came to stand beside her. He gazed down at her as if wanting to say something, but instead licked his lips.

She spoke first before taking out the next ingredient. "So what do you usually do for a job?"

He knit his brows and pressed his lips together. Then he rubbed his hands as if they were dirty, shuffling his feet along the floor. "A bit of maintenance work here and there, you know. It gets me out of the house."

Oh, sure!

"Does it pay well?"

Gregorio watched her closely then sniffed. "I suppose I do okay."

"And today you're not working?"

His face reddened. "What's with all these questions?"

Valeria moved back to retrieve a jug of milk. She took a few deep breaths, realising she might've overstepped her boundary. She had to keep things neutral. It wasn't like she knew what he really did to get money. She was just assuming it wasn't anything good or legal. "I'm just making conversation."

He stepped closer into the kitchen, inches away from her. His body odour, a rank musk that made her suck in her breath, moved her back a step. She moved away and began to mix the ingredients, but her body shook. Her hands lost their strength as she mixed the flour in with the sugar.

He leaned in closer. "Do you want any help?"

"No thanks. I'm good. You can go and relax."

Gregorio crossed his arms and continued to gaze as if contemplating what to do next. Then he nodded and walked down the corridor. Thank god he was gone. How could Alessandra be having a relationship with him? Her friend must not know what she was getting into.

Valeria finished baking the biscuits, then pushed the trays into the oven. The sudden rush of heat caused her to feel dizzy. Stumbling away from the scorching heat on her cheeks, she tripped over a rough part of the floor and crashed head first into the tall cupboard. Not again, she thought. How could one girl be so clumsy? She was dimly aware of the crack of her head against the wood and rattle of dishes inside. Then a wave of blackness fell over her, and she knew no more.

Valeria opened her eyes, a raging headache pressing into the back of her skull. A blurry figure bent over her, and warm, stubby hands cleansed her forehead with a face washer. The damp heat of the water and the softness of the cloth against her aching skin felt comforting. What had happened? The last thing she remembered was baking biscuits, then she must've tripped. Who had found her? Was it Giovanna or Gregorio?

The blur coalesced into Giovanna's squat figure. "Oh, thank god you're okay. How are you feeling?"

Valeria pressed her hand against her forehead to fight the stabbing pain. She felt dried blood around her temple. "A bit sore, and a bad headache."

"The doctor's coming to see you in a little while, but your family's not home yet. We'll tell them later what happened."

She leaned her back against the bed. Was it Giovanna's room? "What happened?"

"Well, I found you on the floor. You must've tripped and hit your head on the cupboard. I think it happened just before I got in. Gregorio helped me get you up but now he's gone out." She shook her head. "That's all he seems to do. Just goes out with people I don't even know. He's not one to stay home for long."

The genuine concern on Giovanna's face made her endearing. Valeria saw her nurturing side as Giovanna wiped her face with a towel and stroked her cheek, knitting her brows and then smiling.

In spite of Giovanna's warmth, the thought of Gregorio touching Valeria made her ill. She was surprised he hadn't left her rotting on the kitchen floor. Maybe he had a heart after all.

Chapter 28

A STEP
TOWARDS
CLOSURE

E nzo scanned Valeria's face, convinced that
something was going on. Something he
wouldn't like. His nails dug into his skin as he
clenched his fists. Valeria sat across from him with
a guilty look in her eye. She was definitely up to
something. He'd have to keep a better eye on her.
One of the villagers had recently mentioned that
Valeria had been seen with a boy named Dario, one
of Ciro's friends. Was there something going on
between them? She might believe they were only

friends, but Enzo knew better. Sooner or later, a boy always wanted something more.

He peered at her closely. "You expect to see Alessandra again?"

Valeria nodded.

"I find her to be a bad influence."

She turned to her sisters and brother, who had lowered their heads to eat their pasta. She picked at her food, looking as if she'd lost her appetite. He'd force her to eat if he had to. "But Papa," she said finally, "we've finished the dress and now this friend might want other clothes."

He sighed. "And why can't Alessandra do that on her own? Why do you need to be there? You never stay home with the family, and today is Sunday, of all days."

Valeria fidgeted and slightly shivered. "I love sewing, Papa."

He angled his head, watching her closely. Was this so-called friend just an excuse to see Dario? She was getting a bit too much freedom for his liking. Maybe he could get Gregorio to watch over her? Yes, that was what he'd do. "Who is this friend? What's her name, and why haven't I met her before?"

He waited for a response as Valeria pushed her fork into the pasta and put it in her mouth. She drank the water, her hand shaking.

Interesting, he thought.

"Her name's Elsa, Papa."

She was lying. He could see it in her eyes, but he'd play along. Maybe Gregorio could follow her today. He'd find out what she was up to, and if she was seeing a boy, she would be punished. There was no way she was seeing a boy at her age—or at any age for that matter, until she planned to marry the man. What scandal would be next? What would people in the village say about her ways? No, he had to control the situation.

He looked at her sternly. "You can go today, but do not make this a habit every Sunday. I won't stand for this, Valeria."

She averted her eyes. "Yes, Papa."

He leaned forward. "And no more accidents with Giovanna. You must be focused."

"Of course, Papa. Can you let Mama know where I'm going?"

He grunted. "She'll be back soon from the shop, so you can tell her yourself."

He watched her leave the table, a spring in her step that reinforced his suspicions. Whatever she was up to, he had to put a stop to it.

He pushed away from the table and went to visit Gregorio.

Strolling down the street and passing by the stores, Valeria took a few deep breaths as she thought about her conversation with her father. He was drilling her as if she was a soldier, and it made her sick. It was as if he suspected something about Dario, but they were over now. It was over before it really began.

She stumbled over a bit of uneven ground, and gasped. What was going on with her? What was it with all these accidents?

Her heart thudded in her chest as she thought about seeing Dario again. He probably didn't even know she'd be there to greet him when he came to pick up his mother's remaining dress fabric he'd forgotten. Alessandra had told her to come by to talk sense into him. Maybe together, they could persuade him to change his mind about them. Maybe Valeria and Dario could start their relationship over again.

As the wind rattled her teeth and her hair flew into her eyes, Valeria cast her mind back to the first time she'd met Dario. He was the love of her life, and she didn't want to lose him. She knew he felt the same way; that he would never just break things off with her. No, something more sinister was going on and she intended to find out what.

Finally reaching Alessandra's house, she knocked on the door and waited. The seconds felt like hours. Her feet scuffled across the ground.

Alessandra opened the door, a serious expression on her face. "Hi, Valeria." She swung the door open wider and dragged Valeria in by the arm. "He's here now. I've been stalling him so you'd come." Once inside, Valeria stood frozen in her tracks, unable to make a further step. "Come on, Valeria," Alessandra whispered. "He's in the living room."

Valeria's heart raced. "I'm scared. What if he rejects me again?"

Alessandra sighed. "He won't, but if he does, at least you gave it a go." She latched onto Valeria's arm and pulled her further forward into the living room.

Valeria's heart throbbed at the sight before her. Dario was sitting on the bench, his mind appearing to be miles away. He turned to the noise, his eyes widening when he spotted Valeria. He shook his head, and his face turned a beetroot red. "What are you doing here?"

Valeria's lip quivered. "I—I wanted to talk."

He rose and cleared his throat. "There's nothing to talk about."

Valeria's cheeks burned and her eyes ached from holding back tears. They spilled down her cheeks as she watched him leave.

Alessandra pulled him back into the room. "You owe it to Valeria to talk. I'll be in my room." With a fierce look over her shoulder, she stalked out.

Valeria held a hand over her chest. When she could breathe again, she touched him on the shoulder. He turned at the touch, his eyes wavering. They looked bloodshot, as if he hadn't slept.

"What's really going on with you?" she said, feeling a pinprick of pride at the steadiness of her voice. "I thought you felt the same way about me as I feel about you."

"It was a mistake," he said, turning away. "There are just too many obstacles."

With a hand on each of his shoulders, she turned him to face her. "Nothing we can't work out."

"Your father," he started, then waved his hands in a helpless gesture. "He would never approve."

Now he was just reaching for problems, Valeria thought. There was more to it.

Chapter 29

A LOVE THAT WON'T DIE

Valeria took a breath. "I know my father wouldn't approve, but I don't have to tell him anything. We can see each other in secret." She flashed him a smile. "It can be fun!"

He sighed. "This isn't just about you and me. It affects other people and I—I don't know how it can work out."

She angled her head. "What other people?"

He looked away, his hands shaking. "Never mind. Just let this go. Please!" He started to turn away again, but Valeria pulled him back towards her. She dared herself to make the first move. With her right hand, she moved his face towards hers. Slowly and deeply, she kissed him, lingering, and felt the softness of his tongue and the warmth of the kiss. Her heart stirred as she deepened the kiss while Dario stroked her neck and hair.

Then he wrenched away. "Valeria, we can't." He drew a long breath, then turned towards the window and looked out as if searching for something.

She forced the hurt from her voice and laid her palm between his shoulder blades. "But…I know you want me. I want you too."

He pulled away, shaking his head. "No, this is wrong. I will not take advantage of you. You're only fifteen, and this cannot go any further."

Valeria sighed, an empty feeling in the pit of her stomach. "We don't have to go all the way. We can enjoy each other in different ways."

Dario gave a rueful laugh. "You're one cheeky girl, aren't you?"

She turned serious. "Are you ever going to tell me who beat you up? Or at least give me a clue?" She waited but nothing came. "I'm starting to think you're connected to the Mafia."

He laughed, but it sounded forced. "Nothing like that."

He stared at her in silence for a few minutes then reached up to touch her face. He pulled her to him and kissed her hungrily, desperately. It was a kiss with loss and longing, and even as her body responded, her heart broke. This would be their last kiss. She knew it.

"I care about you, Valeria," he murmured, "and I always will, but—but this can never work out."

As the front door slammed behind him, Valeria began to shake. *I care about you, Valeria.*

He cared about her. Whatever was going on, that hadn't changed but he was leaving all the same. How could she stand to lose him?

Chapter 30

REFLECTIONS

I t had been a month since she'd lost Dario, and Valeria had to get out of the house. She told her mother she was going for a walk, then went out into the village. Valeria wandered past the monument and crossed the bridge, lost in thought. She passed a donkey tied to a post near a building, then paused to watch women embroidering on their steel-enclosed balconies. The hanging plants above their heads gave a splash of colour to the stark walls behind them. The sunshine warmed her face as she viewed the distant green mountains, and the lush, towering trees amidst stone and concrete houses.

She felt almost comforted by watching people pass her by as she strolled but kept her head down, pondering her loss of Dario. He was gone, gone for good, and her heart ached as she remembered his lips on her lips, his strong hands wrapping her waist, and the way he stroked her neck and toyed with her hair. She missed him already. He was her missed opportunity. Could she really move on and focus on other things? Her heart wouldn't let her. Not when his image permeated her brain and touched her heart.

He'd told her he cared, so that wasn't the issue. What held him back? He'd witnessed something and been warned not to tell, but why should that affect their relationship? She frowned. What if whatever it was might put her at risk? Dario was protecting her in some way, but she could stop the threat and win him back. She had to at least try.

She found an inviting tree and sat on the ground beneath it, listening to the birds chirping, the sound of cars driving by, and women screaming at children. Bowing her head, Valeria closed her eyes and took deep breaths. She suddenly had hope that she and Dario could make it work if only she could dig for the truth.

She lifted her head at the sound of a voice in the distance. It was Alessandra scurrying towards her, out of breath and planting her hand across her chest. She plopped down in front of Valeria, then frowned and tilted her head as if she had a question. "I went over to your place, and your mum told me you went for a walk. Are you okay?"

Valeria nodded, then shrugged. Was she okay? She wanted to feel hope but her heart still felt numb. "I'm fine."

"Well, you look tired. I mean, I know that you and Dario—"

Valeria gestured with her hand, cutting her friend off. "Give it a rest, Alessandra! I said I was fine."

Alessandra pursed her lips and turned away, silence resounding for a few minutes. "You know, I saw Ciro the other day and he looked really rattled about something. He was walking with his hands in his pockets, ignoring the people he usually greets. It was weird, like he had something on his mind. He was rushing off somewhere." She swallowed. "When I asked him where he was going, he said to leave him alone and mind my own business. He was stressed about something."

Valeria didn't really care about Ciro, but she made herself answer anyway. "Maybe he cares about you so much, he can't face you."

Or maybe he was trying to protect Alessandra. It made sense. Ciro had seemed as taken with Alessandra as Dario had been with Valeria. Yet, both boys had ended those relationships after Dario had been attacked. Ciro had been hurt too, Valeria remembered. She couldn't believe she hadn't put it together before now.

Alessandra gazed into the distance and rubbed her eye. She shifted her legs on the grassy ground and watched Valeria closely. "I think there's something going on, Valeria. Even with Dario. They're hiding a secret and I'd like to find out what it is."

Valeria started to share her suspicions with Alessandra, but she was afraid her theory might not hold up to inspection. Better to be sure before she said it aloud. Instead, she lifted her chin and issued a challenge. "Why are you with Gregorio when you obviously still care about Ciro?"

Alessandra sat silently, biting her lower lip.

"I mean, he's too old for you, and—"

Alessandra suddenly came to life, clasping her hands in front of her. "And what?"

"Nothing. Just forget it!"

With a sigh, Alessandra asked, "What is with you? I feel there's more going on than just Dario."

Valeria drew in a long breath, then plunged in. "I think there's something going on with Gregorio. I saw him with a whole lot of money in his drawer when I was at Giovanna's house. It has to be something dodgy." Alessandra didn't say anything. "Doesn't that bother you? I mean, you're involved with him."

Alessandra averted her eyes. "I'm just having fun. Nothing serious." She turned back to her friend. "But, let's change the subject, okay?"

Valeria shifted on the ground, picking at the grass. The wind played with her face.

"I heard from your mother that Giovanna's going to invite the whole village of Laurino to celebrate her birthday."

Valeria smiled at the thought. Ever since the accident, Giovanna had been much kinder. Valeria almost found herself liking the old woman. "She's having it at the farm. Her house is just too small for all the villagers. Are you going?"

Alessandra looked away. "I wasn't invited but your mother said I could easily go with you. She said that Giovanna wouldn't cause a scandal by telling me to leave."

"I'd love for you to come with me."

Alessandra nodded. "Maybe Dario and Ciro will be there."

Valeria tried to ignore the leap of her heart at the thought of Dario. "Maybe. Won't it be awkward for you seeing both Ciro and Gregorio there?"

Alessandra thrust out her chin. "I don't want to talk about that. I'd rather hear about Giovanna. You're finished with the errands at her place?"

Valeria nodded. "I finally am, but funnily enough, she's grown on me. She's not so bad, friendly even."

Alessandra smiled. "Who would've thought?"

Valeria almost felt sorry for Giovanna to have a son like Gregorio. She was almost certain he was doing something illegal. What if it was something that might hurt Giovanna? A few weeks ago, the thought wouldn't have bothered her, but now she worried for their neighbour. She would have to do some detective work of her own and find out what, exactly, was going on. Between Dario's secrets and Gregorio's she was going to be a very busy girl.

Chapter 31

CELEBRATION ALL ROUND

Valeria and Alessandra linked arms as they ambled towards the farm. The sun cast a glare on Alessandra's face as she gazed ahead in silence. Something was worrying Alessandra, and even though she'd refused to discuss it, Valeria suspected it was about having both Ciro and Gregorio at the same place. She must've agreed to this party because she loved drama and challenges, and this was one.

The wind feathered Valeria's skin and ruffled her hair. She smiled at the sensation, then gasped as her foot sank into a patch of boggy ground that soaked her sandals to their soles.

She grimaced and pulled her foot free, then hurried to catch up with her friend. Further ahead, the trees and bushes whooshed in the breeze, and her breathing grew erratic from the increasing quickened pace. As the farm came closer into view, she saw that already, groups of people lingered or helped to set up tables with her sisters and parents. Valeria's mother had talked her father into letting Valeria help out later after picking up Alessandra. Very occasionally, she was able to do that.

Alessandra turned to Valeria. "We're finally here."

Valeria found it so peaceful in this part of Laurino, with its rivers, towering trees, and bushes, that she almost didn't want to leave. After a while, though, she'd want to get back to the land of the people and keep busy. "Are you okay? You look worried."

"I have to see both Gregorio and Ciro, so it's going to be awkward."

"Just keep your distance from both of them. Stay with me for the night."

Once they reached the guests, Valeria and Alessandra kissed the men, women, and children of the village on both cheeks. They watched as Emilio and Elena kicked a ball around and Carla placed napkins on the table. Valeria's father huddled around a group of his friends, laughing and chattering about his next plantation. Spotting Gregorio beside her father made Valeria's stomach twist into knots. He leaned in towards her father as though he was God himself, nodding and laughing in response to the chatter. She turned away when her mother approached with a grin and a kiss to both girls.

"Come help with the pizzas, girls." Her mother waved them towards the shed.

They wandered over to the shed where Giovanna sat at the table, preparing a pizza. She looked up when the girls entered, then clucked her tongue when she saw Alessandra. "Valeria, so good to see you."

Valeria leaned in and kissed her on both cheeks. "Happy birthday, Giovanna."

Alessandra pretended not to notice she'd been slighted. "Happy birthday."

Giovanna grunted and turned her head back to her pizza.

Valeria gave her friend a reassuring smile as they watched women huddled over dough and oven trays. A few women with scarves over their heads spread the dough with tomato sauce, sprinkling cheese and salt over the pizza, as well as slices of potato, onion, Italian sausage, bocconcini cheese, and peppers. Then one of the bulkier women from the neighbourhood poured enough olive oil over the pizza to feed a third world country. Some of these women loved their oil but it sickened Valeria to see the pizza drowning in a pool of it.

Valeria and Alessandra each grabbed a clump of dough, then made some room on the long table. With vigorous hands, they worked the dough and pushed it flat. Then Valeria added tomato sauce and cheese, with a hint of basil. She poured over a pinch of olive oil then put it aside for the oven.

Once a couple of pizzas were ready, Valeria and Alessandra cut them up, spread them out over worn trays, and then passed them around the table of guests. The smell of basil and fresh sauce gave Valeria hunger pangs as she watched the guests bite into the thick pizza. She had to wait for hers.

Her heart did a flip when Dario and Ciro suddenly showed up at her side and greeted everyone. Dario and Ciro nodded curt greetings to her and Alessandra, then hurried off with stiff postures towards the men's only area.

A mere nod and not even a friendly hello. Alessandra turned pale and quiet, rushing back to the shed while Valeria stared after Dario who kept looking back over his shoulder. She remembered her thought that he was simply trying to protect her, but if that was the case, why were they so detached and cold? It was as though both Valeria and Alessandra had meant nothing to them. If that was really what he wanted, though, she would do her best to pretend.

Alessandra must have come to the same decision. She and Valeria listened and laughed at stories of the older women in the village while the men kept rein in their isolated area. As Valeria dug into the continental cake, Giovanna approached and sat alongside her with a subtle smile.

"I want to say sorry for the way I've treated you, Valeria."

Valeria lifted her head up from the dessert. "There's no need."

Giovanna leaned in closer. "I realise how hard you work, and that you're definitely skilled in many areas. If only my son was a better man, I would've loved to have you as a daughter-in-law."

Valeria suddenly felt suffocated, her throat tightening up. She had no response to that, but smiled to hide her nervousness. Where had that comment even come from?

Giovanna plucked at her skirt and sighed. "I know that Gregorio's only living with me for my inheritance. My other children don't seem to care about the money or me but I know he does. That's the only reason he's here. He's hoping to butter me up so he can get a share of his money now. Otherwise, he'll have to wait until I die to get his share."

Valeria's heart skipped a beat. *What!* So that was the reason he had moved in with his mother. Not to spend time with her or help her around the house, but for the money. *What a horrible man!*

Giovanna excused herself, then rose to leave while Valeria glanced around. Near a towering tree, at the edge of the clearing, Dario, Ciro, and Gregorio huddled closely together. Gregorio scowled and gestured angrily in their faces. Then, almost before her mind could register it, Gregorio slammed Dario against the tree. Valeria's breath caught in her throat. Ciro pushed in between, but Gregorio shoved him to the ground. Dario seemed to wilt under the weight of those large hands as they pressed his body deeper into the trunk of the tree.

She had to do something. Fists clenched, Valeria ran towards them, her breathing accelerated and her feet sliding on the soggy dirt, loose pebbles, and grassy ground. Time seemed to slow down.

Gregorio gave Dario another shake then loosened his grip. Dario fell against the tree, gasping for breath. Then he turned and prodded Ciro away. With anxious glances over their shoulders, they bolted away from the party and back towards the city.

At the pounding of Valeria's footsteps behind him, Gregorio lifted his head. Her palms slammed into the centre of his back, and as he spun to face her, she took a step back.

His smile was ugly. "You don't want to mess with me, Valeria. Get out of here, now!"

For a moment, she felt rooted to the ground. Then she backed away, her body tight and her hands shaking as she felt his wrath. The dark, soulless look in his eye was enough to scare a grown person, let alone a teenager. *What was going on?*

Chapter 32

DISCLOSURE

At the farm the next day, Enzo sat on a crate and waited for Gregorio and his other friends to arrive to finish building the cowshed. He was sipping an espresso that Graziella had brought over to him, the steam rising in swirls above him. His buttocks ached from the firmness of the crate, and to relieve the pressure, he shifted his weight from one haunch to the other, then squinted into the sun. It was nearly halfway across the sky. *Where were they? There were things to do.*

He sighed and drank in the last drops of coffee that warmed his stomach and filled him up before lunch. Time to get moving. He set the cup down on the crate and rose. He yawned and stretched, then strutted around the partially built cowshed to sort out the tools they'd need.

He hefted a hammer, testing its balance and weight. Then, with a few nails in his hand, he banged down hard on a beam, huffing at the lateness of the others. Why did people always have to irritate him or make him wonder what was going on in their heads? He couldn't figure them out. Even his own daughter was a mystery to him. He shook his head at the thought.

Last night at the party, he had noticed how both Valeria and Alessandra had left the party quite suddenly. If he had noticed earlier, he would've grabbed Valeria by the ears and shoved her back into the shed to help with the cleaning up. At the thought of her rudeness in leaving early, he frowned and gave the beam another whack with the hammer. Didn't she know her behaviour reflected on him? Then today, she had the nerve to ask to stay home because she wasn't feeling well. If it wasn't for Graziella, he would've given the girl another belting, but his wife had convinced him that Valeria hadn't slept well and that she might've eaten something at the party that didn't agree with her.

His mind drifted back to Gregorio, who had promised to give him new information about Valeria. They had made that agreement awhile back, but so far, he hadn't heard much. Was Gregorio holding out on him? The thought that he needed a relative stranger to tell him about his own daughter made his cheeks burn. She must be up to something she knew he wouldn't approve of. His scowl deepened. If she was, he would find out, and she would suffer the consequences. She'd never have the luxury of staying home or doing her sewing, or even spending time with Alessandra.

Last night's events puzzled him when he'd spotted Gregorio huffing about later in the night. When he asked what was wrong, Gregorio dismissed him and walked off. Was it Valeria who had done something to upset him or was it Giovanna? Enzo knew that Giovanna treated the young man harshly, which wasn't the right role for a woman. Gregorio should put her in her place. Still, it was their business to sort out. Enzo wouldn't get involved in their affairs.

Enzo recognised the anger lurking in Gregorio. The young man looked like he was about to explode. For a moment, doubt made Enzo waver. Was Gregorio a man you could trust or was his charm a part of a facade? Would he stick by his promise and tell Enzo the truth about Valeria or would he twist the facts for his own benefit?

Enzo bent down to pick up a nail, then straightened when a muffled voice behind him said, "Enzo, how are you doing?" Gregorio approached with a swagger and shook hands with Enzo. His handshake was firm. "The guys will be here soon. Said they needed to pick something up in the village."

Enzo nodded. His eyes pored over the younger man, curious about his sudden change of mood. Yesterday, he'd looked enraged but today he was cheerier than a sunrise. Enzo crossed his arms. "I saw you talking to Valeria last night. You're too old for her."

Gregorio's expression darkened. He turned away briefly. "I'm not the one you should be worried about."

Enzo turned to him. "What are you talking about?"

"She was seeing this Dario guy, but apparently, they're not seeing each other anymore. She's heartbroken."

Enzo's face reddened. His chest squeezed. His breath came in bursts as he clenched his fists, then dropped the hammer. "What the hell are you talking about?"

Gregorio drew back. "What do you mean?"

Enzo leaned in closer, pressing his lips together then biting his lower lip. "How the hell could you let her near a boy—"He tried to get his breath back, flexing his fingers and arm muscles. He started pacing and drew a breath. "You know I strictly forbid that sort of thing. It shouldn't have got that far." He paced. "Why the hell didn't you tell me this sooner?"

Gregorio didn't back down, but the pitch of his voice rose. "I'm sorry, but I don't think anything really happened. They were just friends. They—they might've seen each other once or twice at Alessandra's house. They were never really alone, Enzo."

Enzo pounded his fists against his thighs. Did he believe what Gregorio was saying? No, he had some doubt, but he'd eventually get the truth out of Valeria. "So why did they stop seeing each other?"

Gregorio averted his eyes and cleared his throat. Enzo's eyes narrowed. Gregorio was hiding something. "I don't know. I think they might've had a fight."

Enzo's body tensed again. "Are you telling me the whole truth, Gregorio?"

Gregorio hesitated. Then he gave a quick nod. "Of course. That's all I know that happened. You don't need to worry, sir."

Enzo nodded. "I'll sort it out with Valeria, don't you worry." Sweat ran from his pores. "Now, I'm wondering what happened to you last night. You looked upset."

Gregorio stared closely, his breath sounding shallow. "Nothing, sir. Just a bit of a disagreement with my mother. You know how she is."

Enzo smiled, but he knew Gregorio was lying. Something else had happened. He'd have to keep a close eye on the slippery young man.

They'd started hammering nails into beams when Enzo's friends headed their way. He ushered them over, but his mind grew distracted as he thought about Valeria. He planned to give her a piece of his mind tonight about this boy, Dario. When he got through with her, she would never want to see a man without his permission again.

Chapter 33

AN EMPTY FEELING

Valeria lay in bed, the blankets covering her face. She couldn't face Gregorio at the farm today so had chosen to stay home. She cast her mind back to the cold, dark glaze over his eyes. It was almost like he wanted to possess her and if he couldn't, he would rip her teeth out. What was going on with him and Dario?

She wondered if she should confront Giovanna about this, but she didn't want to stir up trouble. She knew their relationship was tenuous at best, so there had to be another way. Now that Valeria had got to know Giovanna, she realised the old woman just needed a voice or a support person in her life.

Someone to be there for her. She'd obviously had many friends at her party, but she still seemed lonely.

Valeria couldn't believe what Giovanna had told her about Gregorio. That he was only after her inheritance. *So sad to think that about your own son.*

With a resigned sigh, Valeria jumped when she heard the door slam. It gave her an uneasy jolt. Had something gone wrong? Had the weather suddenly changed?

The sound of footsteps drew closer. Heavy footsteps, not like her mother's or sister's at all. Her breath froze in her throat. Then her bedroom door smacked open and quivered on its hinges. She shrank against the headboard as her father stormed into her room and flung the blankets off her. A vein in his neck pulsed. Her mouth moved in an attempt to cry out, but her voice seemed to have deserted her. *I'm going to die! Someone help me!*

He slapped her hard across the face. Valeria drew back, gasping for breath, her cheek stinging. Then he swung back his arm and struck her across the other cheek.

With a sickening thump, her head hit the headboard. Her cheek burned, and her eyes swam. The man in front of her blurred as a mist fell over her eyes. For a moment, she felt frozen to the bed. Then she rolled out the other side and dashed for the living room.

With Enzo at her heels, she rattled the front door, her sweaty palms slipping on the knob. She had to get out of here. Now! The weakness in her legs made her stumble as her father grabbed her by the waist. He pulled her back. Her body went numb, her voice gone. What had she done that was so bad? A whimper escaped her. She couldn't bear another beating.

Her father grimaced as he leaned in. "You dare disgrace me again." He shoved her on to the bench. "This time I have my facts straight."

The emptiness in the pit of her stomach helped her voice her pain. "What have I done?"

His flinty eyes stared back at her. *He hates me*, she thought suddenly, though she didn't understand why that should be so. A shiver ran through her, and she shrank away. Then he lifted her by her blouse. She heard the cloth rip as he threw her onto the ground. Her head struck the corner of the bench, and she cried in pain. He was going to kill her.

He stepped towards her, taking his time, enjoying her fear. It wasn't fair. A sudden surge of frustration and anger shot through her, and she kicked out as hard as she could, catching her father squarely in the stomach. He gasped, falling onto the bench. He pulled himself up quickly, teeth clenched, as she scrambled away. "How dare you fight me? You have no honour."

He leaped towards her and yanked at her hair. Valeria flailed with her hands, striking him across the face. He didn't flinch but grunted, then grabbed her by the shoulders and squeezed hard, a pinching pain causing her to flinch.

He was looking at her differently now, like she didn't exist, as if his mind was glazed. In that moment of distraction, she shoved him away and bolted to her room. There was no lock, so she leaned against the door, her breath coming in ragged bursts. A few minutes later, she felt his body pressed into the door. She pressed harder, pressed until her arms trembled with the effort, but she was no match for his greater strength and weight. The door crept open, then burst forward, throwing her back against the bed.

As he came at her with his belt and fists, she covered her face and curled around herself. Her mouth filled with blood, and her nerves shrieked with pain. As she slipped towards unconsciousness, voices in the distance drew closer. She dropped to the floor, hands falling at her sides. She was too weak to fight him anymore.

Then a figure shoved her father away and the beating ceased. She squinted up through swollen eyes and the faint image of her mother and Carla became clear.

"Stop it, Enzo! Please stop!" her mother said.

"Papa! You've done enough," Carla said.

He blinked rapidly. "She has to be punished."

Graziella neared him. "Calm yourself down! She's hurt. Can't you see that?"

As if he had come to his senses, he drew back, then turned and stormed out of the room. Footsteps resounded in the distance, and the front door of the house slammed.

Valeria bowed her hands over her head. She closed her eyes and shut out the nightmare of the violence, the belt, the rough hands. She felt nothing but shame; shame at not being the kind of daughter her father wanted. With that shame came sadness and hurt. Was she a dirty object to be discarded? She was nothing to him. Not a daughter, not even a human being!

She opened her eyes. Her mother pulled her up and laid her in bed. Carla left the room, then returned with a bucket and wet cloth. She sat alongside the bed and dabbed her cheek that felt hot and stung.

"Oh, god it hurts!"

Carla stopped for a moment. "I'm sorry."

Her mother watched closely then stroked her hand and kissed it. "I'm sorry you had to deal with this again. You shouldn't have to."

Valeria wiped away her tears. "It's okay, Mama. You weren't to know."

"I had a sneaking suspicion he was angry about something after he spoke to Gregorio. I decided to leave shortly after he did. I'm so glad I did."

Valeria's heart tightened. "He could've killed me, but I don't know what I did."

Her mother sighed. "I'll have a talk to him, but one thing I'm certain about, Valeria."

She tilted her head. "What's that?"

"You can no longer live here under this roof. It's not safe for you anymore. She frowned, as if considering. "What do you think about going to Alessandra's house for a while?"

Valeria felt an ache in the pit of her stomach. She stared at her mother, trying to understand. Her mother wanted to send her away? But why? Did she think this was Valeria's fault?

The thought that her mother might abandon her too was almost too much to bear.

Her mother didn't wait for a response. "I'll speak to Alessandra, but in the meantime, you can't let this experience defeat you. You are strong and resilient, and I know that in spite of your hardships, you'll always win out in the end. It's just like dancing in the rain. You'll always win out in the end. There will always be rain, dear one. We can choose to stay inside and cry about it, or we can go outside and dance. I believe you will choose to dance. Always remember that, Valeria."

Chapter 34

A MILESTONE

V aleria turned sixteen two weeks after her father's beating. She was staying at Alessandra's house, but for today she was back home. Her mother had brought home a cake from the pasticceria.

While Mama jiggled candles into the centre, Carla grabbed napkins and set the table for an afternoon gathering. Valeria felt a chill in the air in spite of the warmer weather, and she wished she could stay in bed all day.

What was the point of having a birthday when her father hated her and Dario was no longer in her life? She hoped she could get through her sixteenth birthday without being beaten again.

As Carla and her mother worked, she slouched in her chair and held back tears. Elena and Emilio played a card game across from her. She bent over the table and spread out her arms.

Her mother turned to her. "Darling. Why don't you go for a walk and clear your mind. It'll do you the world of good."

Valeria nodded and sullenly rose, shuffling towards the front door. A whiff of cold air brushed her face as she closed the door behind her. She almost tripped on the cracked concrete as she rushed ahead, trying to avoid the stares of the neighbours seated in front of their homes. As always, they appeared to enjoy the views.

The mountains in the distance always gave her perspective as she realised it was a part of her journey to feel this way. She was growing up and having emotions she didn't truly understand, and it unnerved her. With the support of her mother and Carla, she could get through anything. It was just a stage in her life.

In the distance, she drew back when she spotted her father strutting towards the house. She passed him without a word, then felt a strong hand pull her back towards the house.

She tried to jerk away, but his fingers clamped onto her upper arm, held fast. "Don't touch me!"

Her father's eyes made a quick scan of the neighbourhood. Then he let her go. "Keep your voice down. Others will hear you."

She shook her head then sighed, averting her eyes. She felt like a mouse in a trap. She inched away from him but he leaned in closer and said, "I will not have your silent treatment any longer. For the past two weeks, you've had your freedom, but I've still kept an eye on you. For now, you can stay at Alessandra's, but I deserve to be acknowledged and respected."

She shrugged. "All because I saw Dario a few times. Nothing much happened between us, but if you took the time to talk to me, you would've known that. Instead, you use your fists before your voice—as you always do."

His teeth clenched but he contained his fury. His eyes covered hers like fire. "You will not speak to me this way. I am your father, Valeria, and I deserve respect."

She chuckled. "Just like you respect me?" She hesitated, then ploughed on. "You believed Gregorio before even talking to me."

He said nothing but pursed his lips and looked away. Valeria saw her chance to head off, jogging on the way to nowhere. She heard her father's voice and footsteps behind her as he followed her, puffing. "Please stop! I'm not finished with you yet."

Did her papa just say please? Was he feeling shame over what he did to her, realising how harsh his punishment was? If so, it served him right. She would no longer be an object he could knock and bully around. She was her own person.

A laneway was up ahead so she started walking through, then stopped, frozen in her tracks. Three men lingered in a huddle. When one of them looked her way, she realised it was Gregorio, a startled expression on his face. He was exchanging money and what looked like bags of drugs with two men. She felt her father's hand on her shoulder, and turned to see his face as pale as a sheet.

"Get out of here. Now!"

Valeria nodded and turned back towards home, glancing over her shoulder. Her father stormed off towards Gregorio. He swung back his right arm and punched Gregorio hard in the face. Gregorio stumbled backwards and fell flat on the ground, groaning. Two stout strangers glanced at each other, then bolted away. They didn't look back.

Wincing, Gregorio sat up and touched the red spot on his cheek. It would almost certainly bruise.

Papa shook a finger at Gregorio. "You will no longer work for me. You're done!"

Gregorio laughed, then launched to his feet and swung a punch at her father. Papa stumbled backwards and landed hard on his tailbone, blood dripping from his nose.

"You pay a pittance anyway for an old man. I never liked you much." Gregorio tilted his head. "I could kill you right now with my bare hands, so go on, hit me again."

Valeria ran towards her father and pulled him up. "Papa, are you okay?"

He stared hard at Gregorio as he rose. "I'm fine." He pointed a strong finger at Gregorio. "You come near my family and I'll kill you. That's a promise." He paused. "I trusted you and now I see you're selling drugs to lowlifes like you. What has become of you, Gregorio? What would your mother think about this?"

Gregorio threw back his head. "My mother! She never cared about me so I doubt she'd worry about this. She's just a miserable old woman who deserves to die alone."

Her father pushed Valeria away. "I thought I told you to leave."

"Not without you."

He turned back to Gregorio. "What happened to you? Why are you doing this?"

Gregorio smirked. "Why do you think?"

Her father started to walk away, then turned back and said, "You're finished in this town. You won't ever work for anyone again, so I suggest you leave. If you don't I'll have no choice but to call the police."

Gregorio's face reddened, his eyes looking cold and empty. "You can't tell me what to do. I don't have to leave if I don't want to."

"Then suffer the consequences."

Gregorio took a step forward. "You don't want to be my enemy," he said.

With a wordless shake of the head, her father took Valeria gently by the arm and walked her back towards home.

Her father was silent on the way home. It was a relief when he opened the front door and gestured her inside. The family and Alessandra were gathered in the living room. Papa grunted towards Alessandra, then stalked into the kitchen area and sat at the head of the table where Mama had placed a steaming pan of lasagna and a salad—a rare treat made possible by the help of the neighbours.

Alessandra pulled Valeria into a tight hug. "Happy birthday, Valeria. You're as old as I am now, so welcome to the sixteenth birthday club."

"Thanks," she said.

Emilio and Elena pulled her into a tight hug, then both sat at the table. Carla set a jug of water in the centre.

Her father gave Valeria a stern look and shook his head. He obviously didn't want her saying anything about what they'd just witnessed. That was fine with her.

Her mother stared. "Are you okay, Valeria? You look a little pale."

Valeria stroked her cheek. "I'm fine, Mama. I'm happy to have my family for my sixteenth birthday."

"I love you, darling. Happy birthday." Mama embraced and kissed her warmly, then took her place at the table.

Papa stood up and reached out to touch her shoulder. He nodded and displayed a tiny smile. She couldn't believe this was the same man who had beaten her twice. The gentle way he had pushed her away from the drug deal and his concern for what she'd witnessed surprised her.

Dinner with Alessandra by her side was heartwarming. She blew out the candles after dinner and made a wish. She wished to be free!

Biting into the birthday cake, an image of the dark look in Gregorio's eyes flashed before her. She wondered if by confronting Gregorio, her father had made things worse.

Chapter 35

A TRICK

E milio stepped out of the concrete building, leaning against a post. He waved to his friends walking in the other direction.

His school bag weighed heavily as he trudged across the dirt ground, heading towards Elena, who was waiting for him on the footpath. He lifted his face to feel the warm wind on his cheeks. The screams and whistles of the other children washed over him as they rushed in all directions. Some of the children were meeting their parents and others walked off in groups. It was like they couldn't get out fast enough, but Emilio liked school. He missed leaving it.

Elena frowned. "Listen, Emilio. My friend wants me to walk her home today." She pointed towards her friend, who was busy shoving books into her backpack. "She has to tell me something. Is that okay?"

"Sure, I can walk on my own. I'm not a baby."

"Just wait for me in front of the pasticceria, then we can walk home together."

Emilio gave her a knowing look. "You just don't want Mama and Papa getting mad."

"That's right, Emilio, I don't. So just wait there for me. I won't be long."

He nodded, then walked off. His bag dug deep into his skin. Maybe it was time for a new bag. The straps were worn out and it was ripped at the seams. He decided to take a different route. Otherwise, he'd have to wait a long time for Elena. It was a little-used path through the bushes that children used whenever they wanted the quiet surrounds, away from the noisy banter of children, without anyone around. It was almost creepy walking the deserted tracks, but at least it would take him longer to get to the pasticceria. He hated waiting.

Emilio lifted the bag off his back and held it with both arms against his chest. That was better! Now he could walk with less weight on his back.

He sauntered alongside the walking track, thinking how nice it was to exercise his legs after a whole day of sitting. The wind cooled his face. Clouds started coming in, and the sun was going down. Would there be rain? He hoped he'd be undercover before that happened.

A rustle in the bushes broke into his thoughts. Then breathing noises came from that direction. What was going on? He squinted into the bushes, where it looked like someone might be hiding. One of the older kids waiting to prank some of his friends. Nothing to worry about. Still, Emilio quickened his pace. He'd just continue along his track. His head shifted when a voice called his name.

"Emilio! Come look at this."

He didn't know that voice. Who was it? An unfamiliar face came out of the bushes. A short, young boy with a large belly smiled, waving him over.

"Who are you?" Emilio asked.

The boy's eyes roamed the area. "I go to your school."

The boy lied. Emilio knew when someone was lying, and this was one of those times. He frowned as the boy went on. "I want to show you something interesting here. I found a load of money. We can go halves."

At the mention of money, Emilio broke into a smile, his suspicion forgotten. His face lit up. *Money!* He always needed money. He wondered where it came from. Who'd leave money lying in the bushes?

His smile faded. "You're lying. No-one would leave money in the bushes."

"That's where you're wrong." The boy pulled out a lira from his pocket. "This was in the bushes. And there's more here. So much more." The boy's eyes explored again. What was he looking at? His hands fidgeted as if he was nervous about something.

Emilio cocked his head, considering the lira. "I always need money!"

The boy waved him over again. "Come and get half of it. I'm happy to share. There's so much of it. We'll be almost rich." He laughed, but it sounded forced.

Why would a young boy want to share the money with a stranger? That didn't make sense. If it was him, he wouldn't tell anybody about it. Not even the police.

Still, what was it people said about a gift horse? Maybe the boy was just trying to be nice. Emilio glanced around and saw a few people in the distance. They were headed this way, but there was still time to get this money then make his way back home.

Elena would most likely take her time with her friend.
There was no rush.

He strode into the bushes, his heart leaping.
Nearing the boy, he looked around the bushes and
found it was empty. No money!

"Where is it? Where's the money?"

The boy smirked. His arm swung, and his fist drove
into Emilio's stomach. Gasping for breath, Emilio
fell back. He knocked his head into a prickly bush,
then flailed about, trying to get up and away from
the flurry of punches. Emilio covered his stomach,
but the boy's fists pounded his hands until they felt
bruised.

"No, stop! Please! What have I done?"

The boy paused for a moment, breathing hard.
"Sorry, this isn't personal."

The boy's arm hung above his face. Emilio cowered
and covered his face, but the boy kept flinging
punches at him. Blood trickled from his mouth and
nose, and from a cut above his eye. Every breath hurt.
Emilio retched and blinked back tears. He had to
fight back.

He dropped his hands, then rolled and scrambled
to his feet, steeling himself against the barrage of
punches to his sides and back. Then he whirled and

flung fists into the boy's face. The boy didn't flinch. His large build made him strong. Emilio's punches were like feathers dropping on his head.

Emilio tried to break free. The boy got him in a headlock and threw more punches into his face and stomach. Salt and copper filled his mouth. His vision darkened and blurred. *He won't stop until I'm dead*, he thought. Or until he'd lost all energy to fight back. His knees buckled and his arms dropped. Then all he saw was black.

Chapter 36

AN UNEXPECTED CALL

Valeria rubbed the sweat from her brow, in spite of the winter chill across her face. Her shoulders ached, and her feet squished in the rich soil. Shovelling into the dirt, she tilled it deeply. Taking seeds out of her pocket, she pushed the carrot seeds into the soil, careful to line them three to four inches apart. She gathered more seeds from her pocket, and set them into the soil all lined up in a row. She couldn't wait to get fresh carrots.

Throughout the winter, her parents usually planted asparagus, winter apples, parsley, chives, and citrus fruits like oranges, lemons, and limes. All year round, they were able to plant whatever was right for that season. She had learned a lot about plants and organic foods, and knew they were lucky to have all of the fresh fruit and vegetables instead of the watery, canned foods.

Her parents were nearby, backs bent, planting winter lettuce. Her father watched her curiously, but her mother forced a smile as if to say 'don't rock the boat'. She didn't plan to do anything but was wistful for her days of freedom. She admired her parents' hard work and tenacity. However, when she looked at her father, the aching feeling of pain and abandonment gnawed at her constantly.

The farm, the quiet, and the natural landscape was a welcome distraction from all that had happened. Valeria was still staying at Alessandra's as her mother still worried about her and said she felt that Valeria wasn't safe staying home. When would she be safe? She couldn't stay at Alessandra's forever. Her mother checked in on her almost every night, bringing homemade food. Alessandra's father was drinking less and seemed to be working through his drinking habit. Maybe it was partly Valeria's influence or maybe he was just sick of the life.

She inched herself away from the soil, trudging to the shed and washing her hands. The water felt cold on her skin as she scraped out the dirt from her nails and under her skin. An anxious young voice resounded outside. Was that Elena?

Valeria left the shed, heading out, and saw Elena clutching at her hair while talking to her parents. Her mother's eyes widened and her father dropped his shovel and rushed away with Elena.

Valeria hurried over to her mother. "What happened with Elena?"

Her mother pursed her lips, then spoke. "It's Emilio. He's been hurt. We should go."

Valeria's stomach clenched. Emilio? Hurt? No! She gave her mother a quick nod, and they ran off towards Laurino, not far behind Elena and her father.

Her mother's hands shook. "Carla will be home soon. She'll find out when she gets home, but at least Giovanna is there with him."

Valeria swallowed, feeling sick to her stomach. Who would do such a thing to a nine- year-old boy? Probably some bully of a student who wanted all the control in the world. She hoped her little brother was okay.

The winter breeze felt like it was hardening her heart as she tried to keep up with her mother, Elena, and her father. It was like running a marathon where she had to get to the finish line. It showed that her parents cared about Emilio. Why couldn't her father care about her that way? What was so different about her that he had to reject her time and time again? A sense of guilt washed over her. How could she think about herself at a time like this?

Stepping across twigs, stones, soft and wet dirt tracks, Valeria almost lost her footing. Her mother looked behind her. "Hurry, Valeria. We want to get to him quickly."

"But Giovanna's with him. He's not alone."

"That doesn't matter. I still need to make sure he's all right."

When they finally reached the house, she settled her breathing. Her hand pressed against her chest. She was aghast at the bruises and scrapes across Emilio's face. He lay on the bench while Giovanna handed him a glass of water.

Her parents neared him. "What happened, Emilio?" her father asked.

Valeria knelt close to him and stroked his face while Elena stayed beside her in silence.

Emilio winced, pressing hard on his stomach. He was obviously in pain. "This strange boy just kept punching me. He was in the bushes pretending he'd found money." He knit his brows. "I believed him. I thought he wanted to share this money he found, but there was no money. He tricked me."

"And do you know why he did that, darling?" her mother asked.

Her father clenched his fists. "Right. Tomorrow, I'm going to the school to find this boy. Do you know his name?" Emilio shook his head. "What did he look like?"

He shrugged. "Probably as tall as me, with a big stomach and short hair."

"Would you recognise him if you saw him again?" Valeria asked.

"I think so."

Giovanna spoke up from the kitchen table. "You know, I could get Gregorio to take him to school tomorrow. Maybe he could find this boy."

Valeria and her father stared at each other, her father gritting his teeth. "That's okay, Giovanna," Papa said. "I've got this. I'll take him to school tomorrow."

"Okay. I just thought he could help."

Mama smiled. "Thank you, anyway, Giovanna."

Papa stared at his son. "Why wasn't Elena with you?"

Elena blushed, tears streaming down her face. "I'm so sorry, Papa. This is all my fault. I just needed to speak to my friend. I told Emilio I'd meet him at the pasticceria. I never knew this would happen. I'm so sorry." She bowed her head, clasping her fingers to the point of turning white.

"I'll deal with you later," her father said.

No, not Elena. He wouldn't dare beat her up, would he?

Valeria watched as her mother began to shake. "Enzo. Please don't do anything you'll regret. Elena won't do this again, will you, Elena?"

"No, Mama. Never again."

"She can help out at the farm for a week in the evenings. No books for her for a whole week. Isn't that a fair punishment, Enzo?"

His eyes wandered, pondering. "Perhaps."

Her mother's body relaxed, a smile directed at Elena. "Now you can start on dinner, Elena. I'll help you in a minute."

"Okay, Mama."

"I'll help," said Valeria. "Then I'll go to Alessandra's."

She was relieved that her mother could help out Elena just like she'd stopped her father from beating her almost three weeks ago. It seemed like her mother was finally starting to come out of her shell to protect her children.

Chapter 37

THE SNAKE

E lena watched as her parents dragged the donkey along, a sack full of olives lashed to its back. Her father's shoulders slumped while her mother secured the bag tightly. They'd told her they were bringing the olives to a factory to make the oil. Some nice olive oil to have with their pasta sauce and pizzas.

Her parents passed the olive groves, a huddle of slanting trees carrying olives with tiny leaves of varied shades of green. Surrounding the trees were tall unsightly weeds and prickly plants, a great area to hide in. The thought reminded her of the boy who had beaten Emilio, and she found herself scanning the brush for the bulking silhouettes of ill-meaning strangers.

Still being punished because of Emilio's attack, Elena was on farm duty so was missing out on a day of school. She hated to miss out on a day of lessons but she knew she deserved it. Emilio was too young to look out for himself, and from now on, she'd make sure to watch out for him.

Sighing, she sat on a crate, glancing around to make sure she was alone. Elena reached into the pocket of her pants and grabbed a thin book with worn ends. She started reading, thankful that her parents weren't around to watch her too closely. She loved her books, and stole moments throughout the day to read a chapter or two of her favourite mystery story. She got joy immersing herself in the different worlds, pretending to be a super spy or a woman with super powers. There was nothing better than reading.

Elena knew she should be working but she would only read a few pages. No harm in that, was there?

She felt like she'd barely got involved in the story when Carla's sharp voice snapped Elena out of her book. "Elena, get to work."

Elena stood and stretched, feeling tension in her buttocks. The sun was fading, and she hadn't realised how long she'd been absorbed in her book.

Carla approached and handed Elena a rake. "I want you to sweep up all those leaves." Placing a garbage bag on the ground, Carla shook her head and walked away. She turned back. "Don't think you can get away with doing nothing around here just because Mama and Papa left. I'll be reporting back to them."

Elena huffed, gripping tightly on to the rake. She put her book back into her pocket. "I'm working, Carla. Don't get so stressed out all the time. Jesus!"

Carla grimaced and stormed off.

Elena raked up the leaves, shoulders slouching. Luckily she wore closed jogging shoes or her feet would've been covered in leaves, stones, dirt, and animal poop. The crunching sound of gravel wore her out but she pressed on by raking the leaves into a pile then shoving them into the bag. She put down the rake and rubbed her aching back. The sharp wind didn't help but she had to keep moving to stay warm.

Looking up at the sky, the sun suddenly came back out. Now Elena felt hot from its rays but ploughed through. Where was Valeria? Probably in the shed cooking lunch. Elena hoped so. She was starving, but she had to finish up here first then maybe she'd eat.

Some time later, Elena stopped raking, tied up the garbage bag and left it. Carla could get it later. Elena was having a rest, and that tree over there looked inviting. Heading towards the bushy tree, Elena yawned then sat under it with her book. She hadn't slept well the night before so felt tired and drowsy. As she was reading, she felt her eyes slowly closing until she could no longer keep them open.

Valeria's voice cut through a lovely dream in which Elena was a super spy in one of her mystery stories. "Oh, Christ! Where did that come from, Carla?"

The shrillness in her sister's voice jolted Elena awake. She rubbed her eyes and blinked until her vision cleared. Both Valeria and Carla stood in front of her as white as ghosts, looking at something on the ground. It was wriggling and gliding across the grass, getting closer and closer to Elena. Her voice stuck in her throat and she pressed her hands to her chest, unable to breathe. A hissing came out of its mouth, and she thought her heart might stop.

The snake had different shades of brown, both light and dark. Its eye had a bright red tinge to it. If she wasn't so scared, she'd be fascinated by the array of colours on its narrow body. Was it poisonous?

"I don't think it's poisonous," said Carla, "But I can't be completely sure. We cannot take any chances, Valeria. Kill it!"

Valeria's eyes widened. "With what?"

Carla rushed away, searching for something near the shed then returned. She held a long stick. Valeria grabbed it.

Elena's eyes felt very still. She didn't know if she was blinking but her eyes watered and her mouth was dry. Her body froze as the snake hissed and slithered over the ground towards her.

"Kill the snake now, Valeria," Carla said. "Now!"

Valeria lifted the stick high above her head and swung it downward, striking the snake with a loud thwack. It twisted towards her and slid away from Elena. Again, Valeria struck the snake hard with the stick. Then again and again until it no longer moved. Was it dead or just in shock?

Elena watched the life slowly suck out of the snake, but she felt sick. Its body was being squished. Valeria was killing it, and Elena didn't know if she'd have the courage to kill an animal. She almost felt sorry for the snake, but it had to be done. The violence of it all. She turned away for a moment, took a breath, then watched again. She felt like she'd throw up but she tried to calm herself down as she swallowed.

The snake moved slightly. Valeria struck the snake a few more times. She fixated on the snake until she was sure it was dead. She watched and waited. When it no longer moved, she rushed over to Elena.

"Oh, Elena. Are you alright?"

Elena shivered, her hands chilled to the bone. "I can't believe that happened."

"It's okay. Let's get away from here. Papa can clean that up later. He should be back before the end of the day."

They headed towards Carla who hugged Elena tightly. Elena shrugged her off. After being such a witch with the rake, now Carla wanted to act all concerned and nice. "Oh, stop it! You're hurting me. I'm alright."

Elena forced the tears away. She could do this. She wouldn't let this stupid snake get the better of her. It was dead now, and she was safe, but why didn't she feel safe?

"I don't know how that happened. We've never had a snake in these parts for years. Where did it even come from?" Carla said.

Valeria shrugged. "The grass wasn't even that high so I'm not sure what attracted it here."

Elena's throat felt dry. The image of the snake was still clear in her mind. Her first day on the farm in a while and this had happened. She wasn't sure she wanted to come back here. What if there were more?

As they headed to the shed, Elena spotted a figure behind the tree in the distance.

"Someone's over there. I saw them. Behind that tree."

Valeria ran over to where Elena pointed and then returned. "I didn't see anyone."

Elena shook her head. She was so sure she had seen someone hovering around. She'd always been told she had a good imagination. All that reading, she supposed. Still, she knew what she'd seen. Her imagination wasn't that good.

Chapter 38

SUSPICIONS

Later that day, Graziella and Enzo arrived at the farm where Elena, Valeria, and Carla sat on crates in deep discussion. Carla gestured with her hands while Valeria hunched over with a shake of the head. Elena sat frozen in her spot.

Graziella angled her head, watching as they neared. She drew a hand through her hair, an uneasy feeling falling into her chest. Why weren't they busy working? Had something happened?

At closer inspection, Elena looked pale, Carla's hands were fisted, and Valeria lifted her head and squinted into the cloudy mist.

As she hurried past Enzo towards the girls, her foot nudged something rope-like. A gasp came from her throat and she stumbled back. A snake! She moved to put herself between it and the girls, then realised it wasn't moving. Was it dead?

She nudged it again with her foot. Yes, thank god. A quick glance at the girls showed they were shaken, but fine. As her heart settled, Graziella turned to Enzo. "Watch your step, Enzo!" She bent to look for the triangular head that would tell her it was poisonous, but it was a flattened, unrecognisable mass.

Enzo knit his brows, staring at the snake. It didn't seem to faze him. "Get me a garbage bag from the shed. We can't leave it here."

"Sure, Enzo. I'll be right back."

First though, she had to check on her daughters. They still hadn't moved. Was it the snake that had frightened them so badly? They looked as pale as bed sheets.

She headed towards the girls. "What happened here today?" Graziella said.

Carla straightened her shoulders. "Valeria killed the snake. It was heading towards Elena. She was asleep under that tree." She pointed to it. "If it wasn't for Valeria sighting the snake, who'd know what would have happened?"

Graziella rushed over to Elena and wrapped her arms tightly around her. "Oh, darling! Are you all right? Can I get you anything?"

Elena shook her head. "Oh, Mama! Stop fussing. I'm fine."

Valeria said, "She's okay now, Mama. Do you think it was poisonous?"

Graziella shivered. "It doesn't appear to be a poisonous snake by the way it looks, but I'm surprised. We haven't had a snake in these areas in years. This is unusual."

"Something must've attracted it, Mama," Carla said.

Graziella shrugged.

Elena blurted out, "I'm sure I saw someone by those olive groves. I think the person was hiding."

Valeria scanned the groves. "I didn't see anyone."

Elena pursed her lips, fixated on the ground. "Well, how do we know someone didn't put the snake there?"

Graziella chuckled. "What are you talking about, Elena? That's ridiculous, darling. Why would anyone do that?"

Elena shrugged. "I don't know, Mama."

Graziella turned to Valeria who seemed deep in thought, her finger touching the side of her temple. Was there something she knew that Graziella didn't? Could someone have actually done this on purpose? Why would anyone do such an evil thing?

Graziella rushed off towards the shed. Rummaging on shelves, she picked up a garbage bag, returned to Enzo then handed him the bag. She watched as Enzo lifted the snake onto the end of a stick and placed it into the bag. His nose screwed up. Enzo put the garbage bag aside. Then he and Graziella walked over to the girls.

Enzo stood cross-armed. "So where did that snake come from?"

Carla explained the situation. Enzo huffed. "If you were keeping an eye on the farm Elena, instead of sleeping, you would've had a chance to run off. Then Valeria wouldn't have had to kill it. Eventually, it would've slithered out of here."

Graziella stood firmly. "But Enzo, surely the snake could've come back."

"That snake wasn't poisonous. Harmless, really. We need to respect all living things, as snakes have a purpose in the village." He sighed heavily. "Now I want you girls to do some more planting then you can go home. That includes you, Elena. No more lazing about or we'll get you out of school sooner than you can say books."

Elena cowered, touching her hand to her chest. "But Papa, I love school. I promise to work hard now."

"Then get up and show me. All of you, now!"

Graziella sometimes wished that Enzo had a milder manner. He was always so abrasive with the girls but more lenient with Emilio. All because he was a boy. Still, she had to respect his wishes as he loved them all in his own way.

Lately, he'd been quiet and a little sad, but all he mentioned was that Gregorio would no longer be working with him at the farm. He didn't explain why, but something bad had happened between them. She wondered if Gregorio had taken a bit too much interest in Valeria. Was that it? Or was there something even worse?

Chapter 39

RELIGIOUS GATHERING

Valeria stepped inside the old church alongside her parents, brother, and sisters, sighting the long brown benches, the altar with its surrounding nativity statues, the intricate designs on the walls of the church, the high ceiling, and the posts attached to the walls.

Sitting on the hardness of the bench, Valeria took in the scene in front and wished she was anywhere but here. It was the same old sermon year after year since she was a child, but her mother wanted to celebrate the upcoming Christmas festivity by attending the evening mass.

Recently, she had moved back home, always being careful not to set off her father. How long could she live that way, trying to please him constantly? Although ever since that incident with Gregorio, her father had been somewhat kinder to her. As if he had wanted to protect her from a bad man. She was comforted by it, but that didn't mean she could let her guard down.

As she watched, people came into the church in dribs and drabs, taking their seats. Elena was yawning, Carla was chattering with her mother, Emilio was dozing off, and her father was greeting people stepping inside the church. He knew almost everyone in the village, a real charmer when he wanted to be.

She grabbed a hymn book and flipped pages, feeling the coolness of the church. Her mother suddenly nudged her as Giovanna and Gregorio entered the church. Valeria waved to Giovanna, then averted her eyes, not wanting to meet Gregorio's fixated gaze. How could she look at him in the same way after the way he'd dealt drugs on the street? Shouldn't she say something to Giovanna? Had her father said something to her? Most likely not, as she didn't seem at all upset with her son. It was evident she still bossed him around as she directed him to a nearby bench at the front.

The church was jam-packed when the procession commenced with a song. The priest stood over the altar and started his sermons. Valeria's mind drifted as the wavering voice droned on in the distance.

When people started getting up for the offering of the bread and wine, she rose to stand in the queue, waiting for her turn. A presence at her shoulder focused her mind, and she realised Dario was standing behind her. He seemed to have appeared out of nowhere. How could she not have spotted him before?

Her heart flipped and her stomach ached for him. She missed him.

He smiled and whispered, "How are you?"

She turned her eyes back to the front. "Fine." Then she quickly turned back, whispering, "What's with you and Gregorio?"

His face went white. "Huh?"

He jerked his head towards the altar, where the priest stood waiting. It was her turn to take the bread. She held out her hands to receive, then walked back to her seat. She turned to watch Dario return to his seat on the other side of the church, his gaze glued on her. It was a look of yearning, a look of longing. He still cared about her. His eyes told her so. He missed her as much as she had missed him.

Maybe they could get together again without her father knowing. If she had to, she'd leave home and stay at Alessandra's for a while longer. The thought lifted her spirits.

At the end of mass, Valeria and her family rose and started for home. The moon was bright, and the streetlamps gave the cobbled streets a warm glow.

Giovanna caught up to them, dragging Gregorio by the arm.

"Wait! Graziella, Enzo! We need to talk."

Her parents turned, her father forcing a smile.

Giovanna rubbed her hands. "I want to know why Gregorio's no longer working on the farm."

Her father's face reddened, but he only lifted an eyebrow and watched Gregorio curiously. Gregorio dragged his feet along the ground, avoiding Papa's eyes.

"I have enough help for now," Papa replied.

She tilted her head. "But why have you got Elena helping out when you don't need it?"

How did she know about Elena? Nobody had mentioned anything about her punishment.

Papa frowned. "How do you know that Elena was working with us?"

Giovanna turned towards Gregorio who shoved his mother, shaking his head. "I—I think I might've seen her leave with you—to the farm, that is."

Her father didn't look convinced. "I'm sorry, Giovanna, but Gregorio will need to look for other work." He averted his eyes. "This is also not the time to be discussing such matters. We can get into it another time."

Giovanna threw her hands up in the air, sighing, then slapped Gregorio over the head. "What did you do now?"

Gregorio blushed. "But Mama—"

Valeria noticed their discussion deepening so turned to her father. "I just saw Alessandra. Can I go and talk to her then meet you at home?"

Her father glared. "Absolutely not! We're leaving right now."

Carla intervened. "I can go with her, Papa."

He sighed. "Why do you need to talk to her?"

Valeria fidgeted and looked to her mother, who got the hint. Her mother placed a gentle arm on her father. "Enzo, let them be young. Valeria works hard and needs a break from the farm occasionally. Let her be a sixteen-year-old." She beamed. "Besides, Carla is with her, and you know how responsible she is."

His eyes were still hard. She could see him weighing it. Finally, he said, "Fine, but don't be late. I'll be waiting."

Valeria raced up the concrete path with its cracked lines and down sloping steps. Tablecloths, towels, and a skirt flapped above her on balconies, secured on a clothes line. She almost lost her footing going down further steep steps as Carla tried to keep up.

"Slow down, will you?"

"Hurry up! I have to see Dario." Valeria thought of the altercation between Dario, Ciro, and Gregorio and wondered again what was going on. It had to do with the drugs, she was sure of it now. Her mind was racing.

Out of breath, Carla said, "W—Where is he?"

"I think I know where he lives, and I need—need to talk to him."

Carla's loud sigh was expected, but she followed anyway.

She was sure Alessandra had mentioned it was near this street. There was a red gate, she'd said, and side steps with well-kept potted plants in front. She searched, running along the houses. Everything looked different in the moonlight, but finally she spotted Dario near his house. He turned to see her running towards him and uttered something to his parents who nodded and headed inside.

He grabbed her hand as Carla looked on. "Why are you here?"

She put a hand to her chest, staring into his eyes. "I—I missed you."

His eyes lit up, but then turned dark. "Why are you really here?"

Carla interrupted. "Valeria, you've got to make this quick."

Valeria nodded. "Okay, just wait over by that tree. Give us some privacy. I won't be long." She turned to Dario. How could she approach the subject? *Just say it straight.* "I saw Gregorio doing a drug deal on the street. Did you know about that?"

A shudder ran through him. Then his cheeks reddened, and he looked away. "Leave it alone."

Her arms crossed against her chest. "I saw you following me a couple of times. Why is that?"

He shrugged. "Just making sure you're okay with us not seeing each other."

She shook her head. "No, it's more than that. Something between you and Gregorio." She laid a hand on his arm. "I'm not leaving here until you tell me the truth."

After a moment, he exhaled and flung his fringe back in frustration. He looked into the distance, his mind seeming to process what she'd said. "Fine, if you must know, I —I guess I might've seen a drug deal too."

Valeria froze. Not Dario too. "And did you confront him about that?" Silence. "I asked you if you spoke to him about that."

"Well, he saw me before I could turn away."

She closed her eyes, thinking the worst. "And then what happened?"

"Well, if you must know—he was the one who beat me up. And he said if I told anyone, he would do worse to you. Are you satisfied now?"

She tilted her head, trying to sort out her feelings. She'd been right about Dario's reasons for breaking up with her, and that made her both giddy that he cared for her enough to want to protect her and angry that he hadn't thought enough of her to try and work it out together. "Why didn't you tell me?" she said at last. "We could have come up with something."

Dario laid a hand on her shoulder. "I couldn't let him hurt you. You don't know what he's capable of."

She thought of how battered Dario had looked after the attack. She'd always had a bad feeling about Gregorio, but she'd never expected that level of brutality. If he was capable of that kind of violence, there was no limit to what he might do. She was at least thankful that Alessandra had broken it off with Gregorio.

Chapter 40

A MOMENT

D ario couldn't believe he was getting Valeria involved. It wasn't right. He was trying to protect her from Gregorio but now that she knew the truth, there was no way she'd let this rest. Knowing her, she'd find a way to bring Gregorio to justice, but how would she do that? She had no hard evidence that he was dealing drugs. It was her word against his.

Maybe her father's witnessing of the event could carry more weight with the police.

"I'll tell you exactly what happened, Valeria," Dario said, casting his mind back to the time he and Ciro had witnessed Gregorio exchanging money for drugs. He recounted the incident to Valeria.

It was by chance that they'd taken a short cut through a small narrow street and spotted the exchange. Gregorio was with a group of two men who looked like thugs. Gregorio noticed them instantly, walking towards them with a swagger and a sneer. They turned to run, but Gregorio grabbed Ciro's arm, so Dario stayed behind. No way would he leave Ciro alone with Gregorio.

The man licked his lips and gave them both a shove. "You haven't seen anything here, okay?"

Ciro raised his hands. "Of course. We're going." He turned to Dario. "Let's go!"

Dario didn't like the idea of Gregorio living so close to Valeria. He was afraid for her, considering what he'd just witnessed. He hesitated and was about to leave when Gregorio lifted his arms and pushed Dario against the wall with the darkest of glares.

Ciro tried to help by grabbing Gregorio's arm, but his thugs pushed him away and held him by both arms. "Please, Gregorio. Let Dario go. We're not going to say anything. Please!"

Dario swallowed hard and forced himself to unclench his fists. He was no match for Gregorio's height and weight, and if he tried to fight back, he'd be in worse shape. Gregorio glared and shook his head, his fingers pressed hard into Dario's cheeks. One of his friends piped up. "You know, my mum saw Dario going to Alessandra's place, and I don't think it was to see Alessandra."

Gregorio's eyes narrowed, and his mouth hardened. "Is that right? Are you still seeing Valeria?"

Dario shook his head. "Of course not."

Gregorio bit his lower lip, then grimaced. "Then why were you visiting Alessandra?"

Dario remembered to breathe. "Ciro was there. I was just hanging out with him." He blushed, shivering in the cool climate. His face felt bruised and his back ached from being pushed further into the cold wall. He didn't like the look in Gregorio's eyes, an enraged look. Why was it his business whether Dario and Valeria were together?

"Don't believe that," his friend said. "He's lying. He's been to Alessandra's more than once. Not just a coincidence that she was there as well."

His chest squeezed. "She was sewing a dress for my mum, that's all. No big deal."

Gregorio turned to Ciro. "Get out of here."

"No, I'm—I'm staying."

Gregorio chuckled. "Fair enough! You asked for it." He turned to his friend. "Luigi, take care of Ciro, and I'll take care of Dario. No permanent damage."

Ciro's face paled. "No, don't. We won't say anything."

Gregorio ignored him and swung a punch at Dario. The blow jarred Dario's teeth and bounced his head off the wall. Through a red blur, he watched Luigi pound into Ciro a few times then push him away with a laugh.

"Get going while you still can," said Luigi.

Gregorio ushered for his two friends to leave. "You guys get going. I'll take care of these losers. The two guys jogged away as Gregorio drew back his arm for another punch.

"No!" Ciro flung his arms around Gregorio and jerked hard.

Off balance, Gregorio shrugged Ciro off and reached into his pocket for a steel blade. He slashed the air between them and snarled, "If you don't get out of here right now, I'll kill you. Then I'll kill your friend over here. If either of you say anything to your girlfriends, I'll kill them too. You get it?" He took a step forward, towering over Ciro. "Now, get lost!"

Dario squirmed out from his grasp to make a run for it with Ciro, but Gregorio yanked him back and shoved him to the ground in a flurry of kicks and punches.

Dario drew up his knees and covered his face with his arms. From far away, he heard Ciro shout something, but the words were drowned out by the roar in his ears and the sounds of Gregorio's fists against his flesh. Blood filled his mouth and ran into his eyes. A grey film fell across his vision. Then the punching stopped, and Gregorio leaned in close. The knife flashed, and a sharp pain sliced through Dario's cheek. Then light slipped away and there was no more pain.

A tug at his arm pulled him back to the present. "Dario? Dario? Answer me."

He blinked, and Valeria came into focus, eyes narrowed with concern. "Are you okay?" she asked.

He grounded himself in the moment, and saw he was safely in front of Valeria. Her palm felt warm as she stroked his cheek. He glanced towards Carla, sitting by a tree with her eyes closed. "I'm fine. You need to go."

Valeria frowned. "Why didn't you tell me about Gregorio? We need to go to the police about that. He shouldn't get away with what he did to you."

Oh, how he loved her eyes. He could live in her eyes forever. He wanted to reach out to her, but refrained. Being with Valeria was dangerous for everyone.

He brushed her hand away. "Leave it alone. He's dangerous. You need to stay away from him."

She huffed. "I should at least talk to his mum. She might be able to do something about it. Maybe if she went to the police, he wouldn't go against her. She's his mother."

He shook his head. "Do not underestimate him. He might be the type to hurt his family. You can't take that chance."

Her hands rested against her hips, those inviting lips pressed together, then parting as she spoke. "What do we do then? Nothing?"

He nodded. "Nothing."

"But—"

Dario touched her lips with his finger. "Sshh" His heart warmed at the softness of her lips, the strong gaze, and the lift of her chin. He leaned in and stroked the bottom of her chin. His hand moved towards her cheeks, then changed direction and tugged at a strand of hair covering her eye. She looked beautiful in the moonlight and he wanted to be with her forever.

Without thought, he moved in and kissed her deeply on the lips, exploring her tongue and resting his hand on the small of her back. She kissed him back with a hunger that stirred up old emotions. He hadn't kissed her like that in a while, and he was becoming aroused and wanting more. He felt cocooned in her arms as she drew her hand through his hair, with a little moan. She pulled away for a moment. "Oh, Dario, how I've missed you."

"I've missed you too."

They were about to resume their intimate encounter when Carla stepped in.

"Enough of that! We need to go, Valeria. Papa will be worried."

A look of desperation filled Valeria's face, and Dario felt an emptiness in the pit of his stomach. Why couldn't their relationship be simple? Who was Gregorio to spoil it? His fists clenched. He had to do something about Gregorio.

Chapter 41

A HEAVY WEIGHT

G raziella sank her feet into the soggy ground, carrying two weathered buckets. She pondered the events of a few nights before, when Valeria had disappeared for almost two hours. Enzo had told her about Dario, and she wondered if she'd gone to see him last night. She knew his mother and felt he was a kind boy, but he was the reason Valeria was beaten the last time. He was the reason she had lived with Alessandra for a few weeks. Now, she was back home but for how long? Pretty soon she'd get itchy feet and leave the family. No doubt about that.

She prayed that Valeria wasn't planning to see Dario again for now. If she did, things would only get tenser with Enzo. The storm around Dario needed to settle. Then Enzo might eventually come to love the boy.

Dario had a good soul and would take care of Valeria. He came from a strong and nurturing family, and was a sweet boy with kind manners who seemed to care for those around him. Valeria needed her freedom to be with someone she cared about, maybe even loved. If Valeria married Dario, she'd be close enough to visit. It would be ideal. Did Valeria love Dario?

There had to be a way to convince Enzo to get to know the boy. Maybe she could invite Dario over for dinner. That way, Enzo could see just how decent a boy he was, and that he could be trusted. She had to make it work for her daughter, or she'd lose her. If things kept on as they were, Valeria would eventually leave the family home. Then who knew how far she might run or whether they would ever see her again? Graziella would do everything in her power to keep that from happening.

A noise behind her interrupted Graziella's thoughts. Was that a rustle in the trees? She turned but no-one was there. She hoped there weren't more snakes lying around, particularly when she was alone.

Enzo and the girls would be coming by later to help, but for now she was on her own.

She set down the two buckets and patted some of the cows wandering around the cowshed. Enzo and his friends had done a good job hanging up those timber posts, adding in the long troughs, and its flat roof. The ground was covered with wood shavings, grassy dirt, and bales of hay.

As the cows drank from the trough and grazed on the hay, she chose one to milk. She patted its flanks, then bent down and washed its teat with the water from the bucket. She gently massaged the teat below the udder until the cow was relaxed and comfortable. Then she pushed the bucket beneath the udder and squeezed the teat gently between her thumb and fingers. The milk spurted out into the bucket. She squeezed and squeezed, knowing this would take a while.

She lost her focus for a moment when footsteps sounded nearby. She let go for a moment. "I'll be with you in a minute, Enzo." With a breath out, she relaxed her tense shoulders and refocused on the job at hand.

Rustling leaves and footsteps sounded again. Graziella let go of the teat, but before she could prepare herself, two hands covered her face tightly. Rough male hands. She fell back and flailed her arms to get free, but another set of hands wrapped her arms behind her. A blindfold slid over her eyes. No, oh no. Not this...

She lurched away, toppling over the buckets, splashing milk and water onto her legs. Her face struck the ground. Dust filled her mouth and nose, making her cough.

Then a crushing weight fell on her. She cried out as something in her ribcage shifted, and a sharp pain shot through her side. *The cow!* The huge, heavy mass bleated and wriggled as if fighting with her. Her back and shoulders sank into the ground as she thrashed. Her palms slapped uselessly at the cow's sides, and her mouth gaped and closed, seeking a breath that didn't come.

With a mighty shove, she shifted the cow's weight, enough to let herself draw in a thin breath. The cow gave an aggrieved moo and scrambled up. One hoof landed hard on Graziella's ankle. The pain was enough to make Graziella scream.

The cow moved off in a clatter of buckets, while Graziella pushed herself into a sitting position and tugged off the blindfold. There was no-one there.

Slowly, she straightened her shoulders and rubbed her back, sitting up to fight the dizziness. She swallowed hard and knew that someone had pushed that cow on top of her. Who would do this to her, and why? She didn't have any enemies—not that she knew of. She hadn't done anything to anyone.

Graziella touched her face and found it sensitive to the touch. It must be bruised. Her ankle was beginning to swell, but she didn't think it was broken. As she scrambled to her feet, she cast around for a weapon. There. The pitchfork. She'd been lucky this time, but she would not be caught unawares again.

Valeria stared into the distance as she wandered to the farm with her father and Carla. She saw her mother sitting by the cowshed, rubbing her feet. The pitchfork was propped beside her.

When they approached, her father quickened his step and asked, "What happened? Why is your face bruised?"

Her mother looked frail and tired. Was she working too hard or had something happened?

"A cow fell on top of me."

Carla leaned down towards her mother, pulling her up. "How, Mama?"

Her father squinted. "How would that happen? These cows are not mad in any way."

Her mother shrugged. "I was milking the cow when some men covered my face and pushed the cow on top of me." As if anticipating their next question, her mother turned away and said, "I couldn't see who they were."

A muscle in her father's jaw pulsed. Then he held out a hand and pulled Mama to her feet. She was favouring one foot. "Go into the shed. Carla will tend to your wounds." He turned to Carla. "You take your mother. I'll be right there."

Valeria watched her father closely. He fidgeted, his eyes roaming the farm. He paced around the cowshed looking for something, his face screwed up as if in thought. He shook his head, then turned to his daughter.

"Something's going on here."

Valeria knew exactly what he'd say. "What?"

He lifted three fingers to show her. "Three events have happened that seem all very suspicious. First, Emilio, then Elena, and now your mother in such a short space of time. It can't be a coincidence."

"So what are you saying, Papa?"

He looked into the distance. "I think Gregorio's involved."

Valeria nodded. "What are you going to do?"

"I'm putting a stop to this right now. He cannot keep doing this to our family."

Valeria had an uneasy feeling. Wouldn't that simply make things worse?

Chapter 42

CONFRONTATION

Enzo stalked into Giovanna's house that evening. He felt like steam was coming out of his ears. His fists tightened as Giovanna swung open the door with a smile. Gregorio stood cross-armed and held a confused expression.

"What brings you by, Enzo?" Giovanna asked.

"I need to speak to your son, but you can watch the performance if you like."

She frowned. "What are you talking about?"

Enzo ignored her. Instead, he fixated on Gregorio, blood rushing to his face. He wanted to kill this man with his bare hands. He wanted to wring his neck and watch the life roll out of his eyes. He wanted this man to suffer an unbearable pain after what he was doing to Enzo's family.

Gregorio flashed a greasy smile. "Yes, Enzo. What does bring you by? How's your adorable little family?"

Enzo's teeth clenched, his body preparing to plunge. Without giving Gregorio a chance to defend himself, Enzo ploughed into him and pounded him hard in the face, then fisted him in the stomach. Gregorio fought for control as he pushed Enzo off him and beat him over the eyes, landing a punch that would probably give him a black eye. They wrestled at the end of the bench, rolling on top of one another until Giovanna intervened.

"Stop this now!" She pulled Gregorio off Enzo, and the two men clambered to their feet, bruised, dishevelled, and out of breath.

Enzo slowed his breathing and returned Gregorio's glare. He still wanted to wipe the smirk off the younger man's face.

Giovanna turned to her son. "Can someone tell me what is going on here?" She glanced from her son to Enzo, waiting but nothing came. "I demand to know what's going on."

Enzo licked his lips, then bit his bottom one until it bled. The rage he felt was almost more than he could control but Giovanna stood between them now. Giovanna gave Gregorio a fierce glare, and after a moment, he pulled up a stool and perched there, still glowering. Giovanna sat on the bench and Enzo joined her. He now had a great respect for Giovanna and she needed to hear the truth.

"Why don't you tell her what it is, Gregorio?" he said. "I'm sure your mother would be interested."

Gregorio's face paled and he averted his eyes. Enzo realised his fear of his mother. He could use that.

"I don't know what you're talking about, Enzo."

Enzo chuckled and looked around the room, noticing how clean it was. "Why don't you tell your mother about your drug deals for starters. How I witnessed you exchanging money for drugs." He turned to Giovanna who was ghostly white. "My best guess is he sells it to some other poor loser and makes a profit. No doubt he has a stash of money in his drawer."

Giovanna looked confused. "Gregorio? What is he talking about?"

"Come on, Mama. Nothing's going on. I was buying some other stuff, not drugs. He got it all wrong."

"Then what are you buying? And where are you getting the money, now you're not working?"

He shrugged. "I've been doing some odd jobs here and there. I'm doing alright."

Giovanna grabbed him by the hair, but Gregorio pulled her hand away. She wagged a finger at him. "You tell me the truth right now or you can leave this house. Do you hear me? I won't be putting up with your drugs in this house."

Enzo watched as Gregorio weighed his mother's words. If he told her the truth, she'd disown him. If he continued to lie, she'd still give him a hard time. A no-win situation.

"He's got it wrong, Mama. I'm not dealing drugs, okay."

Enzo was impressed with his lie. The boy looked so sincere that Enzo almost believed him.

"I'll be keeping a close watch on you, Gregorio. Don't think I won't."

Enzo braced himself for the next part of his message. Giovanna had a right to know that her son was a liar and a manipulator who should just leave town.

"There's more, Giovanna."

She sighed. "What more could there be?"

He didn't want to hurt her but Gregorio had given him no choice. He was a man who couldn't be trusted, and Enzo would kill him before he continued to hurt his family.

"I let him go from the farm because of what I witnessed with the drugs. Then, a number of events have been happening." He went on to explain what had occurred with his children and Graziella. Giovanna held a hand to her heart, her eyes softening.

"I am so sorry. Are they alright?"

Enzo nodded. "I believe that Gregorio is responsible for all of these events. A way to get back at me for losing his work at the farm. I am convinced of it." He turned to Gregorio. "I want to hear it from your own mouth. Did you orchestrate all of these events? Is someone helping you out and stalking us?"

Gregorio stood white-faced and remained silent.

"Answer me, dammit. Don't try and look there all innocent."

There was a hint of a smile. "You have it all wrong, Enzo. I don't know what you're talking about."

He swaggered to the door and pressed his lips together. "Just leave."

Giovanna bowed her head. She said nothing.

Enzo left with a heavy heart. If he had a shred of evidence against Gregorio, he'd go to the police. He was no closer to getting to the truth, but he knew without a doubt that Gregorio was responsible. He could see it in his eyes.

Chapter 43

LONG WALK IN THE MOUNTAINS

On Sunday, Carla straightened her shorts and waited for Valeria outside the house. The rest of the family was visiting friends in a neighbouring village, and their father had agreed that Carla could take a walk into the mountains, so long as she didn't go alone.

As Carla scanned the street, she noticed a boy leaning against a post. Was that Dario? She squinted in his direction. Definitely Dario, and he seemed to be watching her. Or, more likely, watching their house. She glanced towards the door, thinking Valeria might step out at any second. No-one.

She straightened her shoulders and started towards him, but before she'd taken more than a few steps, he pushed away from the post and hurried away. Carla scowled and shook her head. He would be wise to stay away, given what their father had done to Valeria the last time he'd found out about them.

Carla's fists clenched. He'd be sorry if Valeria got hurt again because of him. They were too young for a serious relationship anyway. Certainly not mature like her and Maurizio.

She blew out a long breath and paced in front of the house, absently returning the smiles of the passers-by. Where was Valeria? There was no reason for her to take so long to get ready. It wasn't like she was meeting Dario. That wasn't happening, not like last time. Carla refused to be caught in the middle again.

The sound of the door closed behind her as Valeria ambled out.

"Sorry, I couldn't find the top I like to wear. Elena must have borrowed it without asking. She's always doing that."

Carla shook her head. "Who cares which top you're wearing? We're just going for a picnic, Valeria. Don't think you're meeting anyone."

Valeria's face flushed. What was going on with her? Was she planning to see Dario after all? Maybe that was why he'd been watching the house. Carla looked up ahead, but Dario hadn't returned. Maybe Valeria had looked out the window and seen him watching her. She must've been dressing up for him. She just hoped Valeria wouldn't do anything foolish.

During their long walk, Carla gripped tightly to the picnic basket and looked out at the panoramic views of the high valley. The steep inclines and uneven ground eventually led them across a medieval bridge, where they paused to look at the view of the Calore River and laurel trees. She loved entering this part of Laurino with its lush vegetation, shrubs, and olive groves. It was like a haven. The distant view of the patchy mountains was vast and cleared her mind, even though the farm was just as tranquil.

They trekked in silence, enjoying the quiet scenery. When they settled on a patch of grass, Carla laid down a blanket and Valeria pulled it flat on the other side. As they settled onto the blanket, Carla reached to take out glasses from the basket. At a rustle behind her, her hand froze above the basket.

"Did you hear that?"

Valeria shook her head. "No, what?"

Carla turned and waited to hear it again, but nothing came. She was probably just still anxious over the incident with the snake, but Papa had taken care of all that. "Never mind. Probably just the wind."

Carla lifted the flap of the basket and took out mozzarella cheese, a container of fusilli with homemade sauce, a plastic container of water, glasses, and cutlery.

As they served themselves on plastic plates, Carla turned to Valeria. "What's with you and Dario? I thought you two weren't seeing each other anymore. You should be careful, Valeria."

Valeria averted her eyes, biting into her pasta, a bit of sauce falling on to her chin. She wiped it with a napkin. "I—nothing. We're just friends. Nothing more."

Carla frowned. Valeria was hiding something.

"It didn't look like nothing. Not after he kissed you that way. My god! Even Maurizio doesn't kiss me like that."

Valeria blushed. "I worry about him, that's all."

"I'm sure Dario can look after himself. What do you have to be worried about?"

Valeria cleared her throat and put down her fork. She sipped water then swallowed as if to ponder the question. "I don't want you involved, Carla. Just leave it alone."

Carla sighed, drawing a hand through her hair. Another rustle came from the bushes. She turned, waited, and watched.

"I heard that too," Valeria said.

"Do you think it's Gregorio?" Carla hated how small her voice sounded. In a bolder tone, she said, "Surely he wouldn't try anything after Papa's little talk."

Valeria's jaw tightened. "We don't have to be afraid of him. Not with the two of us."

Carla gave a quick nod. They both rose and headed into the bushes, towards the noise. They stepped through the bushes just past a group of tall trees. There was a footprint, a shadow. Carla grabbed a sturdy stick and parted the brush with it. Dario! Stalking again!

Dario came out of the trees. "Busted," he said sheepishly.

Carla threw her hands up in the air. "What are you doing here? Spying on us?"

Valeria looked at Carla. "Yes, I'd like to know that too, Dario."

He started to rise. "I'll get going now. You girls seem to be having a nice time."

Carla pulled him up. "Not so fast! You tell us immediately what you're doing here and why you were watching our house. How long have you been spying on us?"

Valeria said softly, "He's been watching over me for weeks now, Carla."

Carla tilted her head. "You knew?" Silence. "Why would he be watching over you?"

Dario stared into Valeria's eyes. Carla could tell he was still in love with her sister. She felt bad for them, but it just couldn't happen. At least not until Valeria was older.

Dario turned to Carla. "I'm worried for Valeria living so close to Gregorio. So—I'm just looking out for her, making sure she's safe."

"What is this about, exactly?"

As he stayed silent for a moment, Carla and Valeria walked over to their picnic blanket and sat. Dario followed them and sat nearby when he turned and gazed at Valeria. Boy, the way he looked at Valeria, with all that love pouring out of his eyes. It broke Carla's heart. What did he have to say for himself? She probably wasn't going to like it.

Dario drew a hand through his hair. "I'll have to start from the beginning, I think," he said. "But this doesn't go anywhere, Carla. Just keep it to yourself."

Carla had an uneasy feeling. Was Gregorio still so upset over Papa forbidding him to work at the farm? Then why target Valeria? She was about to find out.

Chapter 44

OPEN WOUNDS

C arla averted her eyes as if to take in all that Dario had disclosed. She felt sick. Was Gregorio really into drug dealing and beating people to a pulp? There was no reason for Dario to lie, but it seemed inconceivable that their neighbour had beaten Dario badly enough to send him to the hospital. This was madness.

Watching Dario, Carla swallowed. "We don't have any evidence of this. There's nothing we can do with this information."

"No, that's where you're wrong, Carla. We have eyewitness accounts from Dario, Ciro, Papa, and me," Valeria said.

Carla chuckled. "This is Italy, my dear Valeria. The police don't have the time or resources to be watching over people. Even if you have hard evidence, he might be able to talk his way out of it. Even bribe some of the police officers."

"Well, what about Giovanna? Doesn't she deserve to know her son's into the drug scene?"

Carla shook her head. "Do not get involved in this, please. Leave it alone, and stay away from Gregorio. I cannot emphasise that enough." She turned to Dario. "And that goes for you too. Stay away from him. It sounds like he's bad news."

"I still have the right to watch over Valeria, don't I?"

Carla sighed. "She has her family. We can take care of her."

Dario looked past her, into the trees, and the colour leeched from his cheeks. What was he looking at?

She turned around, and her stomach quivered. She laid a gentle hand on Valeria's arm and realised her sister's hands were shaking.

Gregorio stepped out of the bushes. While the others stayed frozen on the blanket, Carla scrambled to her feet. She approached Gregorio, holding her hands up in the air. "What are you doing here? Have you been following us?"

Gregorio's eyes looked sombre, but his mouth smiled. He ignored Carla and headed to Dario, who launched to his feet and stepped back. Gregorio strutted closer until his face was inches from Dario's. He fixed his gaze on Dario's flushed face in silence then broke out in a laugh. No-one said anything. They were mesmerised by Gregorio's evil laughter and intimidating swagger.

He took a breath and licked his lips, then turned to Valeria. He walked over to her, sat down beside her, then took her hand. Valeria snapped it back. His eyes fired up and his teeth clenched.

"I'm your friend, Valeria. Don't turn away from me. I would never hurt you. You must know that."

Dario rushed over to Valeria and knelt behind her, wrapping his arms around her from behind. At his touch, Valeria's eyes lit up. She turned to Dario with a smile then turned back to Gregorio. "What do you want?"

He placed his hands on his hips. "I heard part of your conversation, and I didn't like what I was hearing."

Carla stiffened. "You cannot expect us to condone your drug behaviour. We won't allow it."

He glared at Carla. "Oh, you won't allow it! What in hell does that mean? Are you calling the police on me?"

Dario shook his head. "We're not calling anyone. I just want you to stay away from Valeria."

"Why's that? She's friends with my dear mum so she's friends with me. Are you afraid I'll get her into the drug scene?" He winked at Valeria. "Valeria's beautiful, so maybe one day, she'll look at me in a different way. I've got time to wait. I'm a patient man."

Dario's hands fisted, his face turning beetroot red. The veins in his temple throbbed and his body shook. He inched his way closer to Gregorio. "You take that back. She'll never want you."

Gregorio laughed. "And you think she'll want you?"

"She'll be mine once we make her father understand what there is between us. Once she's older, she'll be mine and only mine."

Valeria smiled, tilting her head to Dario. "Really?"

Dario nodded. He took her hand and stroked it, eyes riveted on Gregorio. "I know we'll be together one day. We just need to be patient."

Gregorio's eyes darkened. Carla turned to him, and said, "What about Alessandra? Aren't you still seeing her?"

He shrugged. "We broke up, but she was good for a little fun." His eyes fixated on Valeria. "But Valeria here's a prize. And she'll be my prize one day."

Carla walked over to Valeria and touched her sister's shoulder. With Valeria sandwiched between Dario and Carla, she felt braver. She had to protect her sister, and not let this madman get to her. If they could get through this and talk to Papa, he could fix this. He could make sure Gregorio left town and never returned.

Valeria fixed her gaze on Gregorio. "Please, Gregorio. Stop this! You know I care about Dario, and only him."

Gregorio said nothing. Before they could stop him, Gregorio launched himself at Dario and swung a fist into Dario's face. Dario stumbled backwards, his face contorting in pain. He fell flat on the ground, his legs twisted in a weird kind of angle. Valeria screamed and pushed past Gregorio, who stepped back. His eyes were cold and hard, and his face was as red as a tomato. He watched Valeria stroke Dario's cheeks and help him sit him up. His eyes slitted and they embraced.

Carla stood up, grabbed a long stick and pointed it towards Gregorio. "You get out of here now. Leave us alone or we will contact the police."

Gregorio grimaced. "Go ahead. They're all in my pocket anyway."

As he swaggered away, Carla turned to Dario whose nose was bleeding over his shirt. Carla picked up a napkin and handed it to Valeria, who wiped away the blood, her eyes tearing up. She shook her head and held Dario who looked despondent. Carla was worried for both of them. She had to talk to her father about Gregorio.

Chapter 45

VENGEFUL ACT

"What do you mean, Gregorio wants Valeria?" her father said.

"Exactly that, Papa. He wants her all to himself, called her his prize. He thinks Valeria will be his girlfriend one day, but she is definitely not interested. She told him so many times, but he refuses to listen."

His nostrils flared and his chest thrust out. Veins popped out on his head.

For a moment, Carla's resolve wavered. What had she done? Had she made a mistake telling him this? Maybe it would only make things worse, but she was worried about Valeria.

He took a long deep breath, then stalked into the kitchen. A steak knife lay on the bench. He stared at the glinty blade as if dazzled by it. Then he stuffed it into his pocket and headed out. Carla stepped in front of him and raised her arms.

"No, Papa. You can't hurt him."

He looked past her. "The damage has already been done, Carla. Step out of my way."

She stood her ground, cross-armed in front of the door. "I won't let you kill a man then be sent to jail. Think of the family."

He shoved her aside, swung open the door, and strode out. Carla followed him with tears in her eyes. Why was she so stupid? She'd never thought he would get a knife. She only expected him to talk to the man, scare him a little, but not kill him. This couldn't be happening.

If only her mother was here. Mama might be able to reason with him, but she and Valeria were still at the farm. Carla followed him but she had trouble keeping up due to her father's longer stride. He burst into Giovanna's house that was unlocked.

Gregorio leaped to his feet, dropping a magazine to the floor. Giovanna rushed in from the kitchen as her father yanked Gregorio around and held the knife to Gregorio's throat. Gregorio's eyes widened, and his whole body shook with fear.

Giovanna pleaded. "No, stop! Enzo, please. He's my son. Tell me what he's done now." She pushed him but Papa shoved her aside.

Carla circled around to stand beside Giovanna, and took her father by the shoulder. "Papa, no! He's not worth you going to jail for. Please, do it for me."

He turned his gaze towards her, as if weighing his options. He pressed the sharp blade into Gregorio's throat, and drips of blood beaded.

Giovanna grabbed her father and tried to wrestle the knife away.

Enzo's eyes narrowed. "Let go, Giovanna. This is my fight, not yours."

"But he is my son."

He shoved her away with a bitter chuckle. "You treat him like dirt and yet you want him to live? You don't have an ounce of respect for your son, not an ounce, and you want me to leave him alone."

She stared at the ground, tears streaming down her red cheeks. "God forgive me. I know it's true, but I never wanted him dead." She made the sign of the cross and whispered prayers. Papa watched Giovanna with curiosity, his face softening.

Carla dared to breathe. Was he thinking rationally now? Surely he wouldn't want Giovanna to lose her son.

Gregorio's face paled, and he closed his eyes as if accepting his fate. He pressed his lips together and stood as still as a windless night.

"You stay away from Valeria," Enzo said into his ear, "or I will kill you. That's a promise."

He dropped Gregorio and stormed out. Gregorio slumped to the floor, drops of blood pouring to the floor.

Carla stayed behind, wrapping her arms around Giovanna. Gregorio sat on the ground in a daze, but suddenly his face hardened. His teeth clenched. He punched hard into the corner of the bench and winced with pain. "Aah! Goddamit. That man's going to pay! He's going to pay for what he did to me."

Giovanna fixed her gaze on her son, shaking her head. She pulled away from Carla. "Don't be stupid! He told you he'll kill you next time. I might not be around to save you."

Carla approached him. "Please, Gregorio, we don't want a war here. Just leave Valeria alone and my papa will leave you alone. If you anger him further, he'll really kill you."

Gregorio said nothing.

Giovanna pointed towards the hallway. "Go to your room, Gregorio, and do not even think about sixteen-year-old girls. Leave Valeria alone."

His eyes brightened. "But I love her. I would never hurt her, not in a million years. I am prepared to wait a year or two until she's old enough. Then we can leave this godforsaken place."

Giovanna rushed towards him and struck him hard across the cheek. "Over my dead body! You will leave that poor girl alone. She doesn't need a man who can't even take care of himself."

Gregorio reared back as if to strike. Then he spun away and his shoulders fell. He shuffled to his room like a zombie. It was clear his mother still had a hold on him, still held all the power. No wonder he had so much anger inside him. It was bubbling mad like a volcano, and Carla was suddenly scared for her family. Especially Valeria.

Chapter 46

DEADLY CONFESSION

On Sunday, a few days later, Valeria and Alessandra were sitting in the kitchen of Alessandra's house, working on a pair of dresses for a family friend. Valeria cut the last of the fabric pieces and said, "I have to tell you something."

Alessandra's scissors paused mid-slice, and she raised an eyebrow.

Valeria knew that Alessandra had no feelings towards Gregorio, and that she wanted Ciro back. That didn't mean it wouldn't hurt to know that the man you were sleeping with really wanted to be with your best friend. How devalued would she feel?

Alessandra still deserved the truth, though. Valeria could never keep secrets from her.

Quickly, as she threaded her needle and unpinned the pattern pieces from the fabric, she told her friend what had happened, including the drugs, the fight with Dario and Ciro, Gregorio's association with the police, and the encounter on the mountain.

"Then he said he wanted me," she finished.

Alessandra stared. "What do you mean Gregorio wants you?"

Now that she'd broached the subject, Valeria wasn't sure how to proceed. She wished she'd thought it through a little better. If she had, she would have realised that, whatever Alessandra felt for Gregorio, it would hurt to realise he saw her as a bit of cheap fun.

Valeria kept her head down, pricking the fabric with the thin needle, and gave a little gasp as she pierced her finger with the point of the needle.

Putting the unfinished dress aside, she rose and turned on the kitchen tap. In self-conscious silence, she let the water stream over her hand until the bleeding stopped, then dabbed on it with a towel and resumed her sewing.

Finally, Alessandra broke the silence. "I know I'm not seeing Gregorio anymore, but he was always fun to be with. I never thought he wanted you—and when you told me how he beat up Dario. My god, Valeria. He put the poor guy in hospital."

"So long as he leaves me alone, he can take his drugs. I don't really care about that, but I do care if he hurts my family or even Dario again. That can't happen, Alessandra."

"So you're going to do nothing?"

Valeria looked up from her needle while Alessandra pinned the back and front of a top with coloured pins. "He said he's friends with the police so it's probably pointless. Beyond that, what could we do?"

"Well, you won't know unless you try. Gregorio's just a talker, and he's probably lying about that."

Valeria nodded. "Maybe." She turned to Alessandra and put the needle down. "Papa's been a bit quiet lately, even Carla. I think something happened with Gregorio but they're not telling me anything. I think he needs to leave town. Go back to where he came from."

Alessandra nodded. "I doubt he'll leave while you're living here."

Valeria gave her a cheeky grin. "Maybe you could speak to him. Out of a favour to your best friend. What do you say?"

Alessandra finished pinning the fabric then started tacking the two bodice pieces together. "I don't know. Then he'll know that I know."

Valeria angled her head. "Do you think he'd hurt you?"

"Not exactly. I mean, I don't know. Let me think about it."

The sound of a knock at the door broke their discussion. Alessandra put the bodice down on the table and pressed it down with her hands, which shook a little. Valeria wondered who was at the door.

Then a familiar voice called out, "It's just me."

Valeria swallowed hard, then gripped the dress and hugged it to her chest for dear life. What was Gregorio doing here? How could she get him to leave?

The front door clicked open, and heavy footsteps sounded on the living room floor. Alessandra gave Valeria a look of apology. She stood by her friend while Gregorio came into the kitchen and took a seat opposite them. He flicked back his fringe and stared. Valeria waited as he managed a smile.

"I'd just like to apologise for the other day in the mountains. I—I didn't mean to hurt Dario then. Can you forgive me?"

Valeria fisted her hands to her side, her legs trembling. Her hands sweated and her face heated up like a furnace. Her throat was suddenly dry and sore, feeling as if she couldn't speak. No words wanted to come out.

Gregorio went on. "I care about you, so I don't want you to think that I would ever hurt you. I wouldn't, Valeria, and—and—I'd like you to keep an open mind about us—in the future." He gave her such a strong look of desire, she felt breathless with worry and fear. Her stomach was unsettled. She could never imagine a life with Gregorio. Her one true love was Dario, and would always be Dario. Why couldn't he understand that?

Valeria looked at Alessandra who couldn't quite hide the humiliation in her eyes. She turned away, but the pain on her face was as clear as day. A rush of guilt swept over Valeria, so she had to fight back.

"That's not the first time you hurt Dario. Or did you forget about putting him in the hospital? How do you expect me to forgive you? You could've killed him."

He turned to the floor, wringing his fingers. His knuckles turned pale. "I'm sorry. I really wasn't myself that day. I was on the drugs and didn't mean to hurt him the way I did."

Valeria shook her head. "That's not the way I heard it. You're lying."

Gregorio's eyes darkened, his lips pressed tightly together. "I'm not. Please believe that I would never do that again. Never. I wasn't myself then. Please, Valeria. It's so important that at least you believe me. I love you!"

Valeria's body shook. Alessandra squeezed her hand and said, "Please leave, Gregorio."

As if he hadn't heard, Gregorio approached Valeria and took her hand. She snapped it back. "Just leave. I can't be talking to boys. My father would kill me."

"Like he tried to kill me the other day?"

Valeria swallowed, tilting her head. "What? Another one of your lies."

He moved back, as if respecting her space. "Ask Carla. It's true. He came at me with a knife but Carla and my mother stopped him. If they weren't there, I'd be dead."

Valeria shook her head. "Can you just go? I don't want to talk anymore."

Alessandra stepped past her and pushed her palms hard against Gregorio's chest. He didn't budge. "Get out or I'll get my father. He's not far, you know."

He lifted his palm in a gesture of peace, but his eyes never left Valeria's. "Just give me a few more minutes, Valeria."

If he wasn't leaving, then she was. Without warning, Valeria darted past him and rushed out the door. His footsteps pounded behind her. She spun around, tears stinging her eyes. "Leave me alone, Gregorio. Stop following! Please."

Alessandra followed behind. "Gregorio, just leave."

"I just want a few more minutes to talk. Then I'll leave."

Valeria shook her head, increasing her pace as people stared after them. A young woman touched her hand as she passed. "Are you alright, dear?"

Valeria nodded and hurried on. Gregorio quickened his steps and grabbed her hand. As she struggled to pull away, he pressed her palm against his chest. "I want to hear that you forgive me. All I want is your forgiveness. I love you so much, Valeria. Please know that. I cannot stop thinking of you. I always see your beautiful face in my mind. Let me kiss you, right now. Please let me kiss you."

As he leaned in for a kiss, Valeria turned her head away, a sick feeling in her stomach. Tears blurred her vision and she felt trapped and voiceless. How could she get out of this trap he'd set up for her? There seemed to be no escape, only more and more pressure. This man would only suffocate her with his love, but she didn't love him. She'd never love him.

As Gregorio continued to rave on about his love, cars whizzed on by. She blanked out until a familiar voice etched in her brain. *Dario!*

"Get your filthy hands off her. Can't you see she's scared of you?"

Gregorio's eyes dilated but he didn't let go of her hand. Dario moved in and pounded Gregorio in the chest. Gregorio shoved him away, but Dario charged back in, kicking Gregorio in the legs and throwing a fist to the face that threw the bigger man off balance and forced him to release Valeria's hand.

Alessandra looked at Valeria. "I'll go get help."

As Valeria scrambled away, the two men stepped apart, panting.

In a huff, Gregorio said, "I only want her to forgive me. I love her."

Dario's eyes had fire in them.

Valeria touched him gently on the chest. "Leave it alone, Dario. Let's get out of here." She didn't like where this was going. It felt like her skin was being pricked by needles. "Let's go!"

Dario shook his head and jabbed a finger towards Gregorio's chest. "You'll never have her. Do you understand that? You will never have Valeria. She loves me."

Gregorio smirked, triggering Dario's fury. Dario swung back his right arm and landed another punch to the stomach. Gregorio grunted and hunched around Dario's fist, then launched himself forward and pounded his fists into Dario's face. Dario stumbled back, blood streaming from his nose. He wiped it away with a sleeve and Gregorio lunged again, landing a punch to the stomach.

"Stop this!" Valeria tried to push between them, but the flurry of punches drove her back. She glanced wildly towards the gawking neighbours. "Someone stop this!"

Her stomach sank as she realised the onlookers were all elderly people and children. What help could they possibly be?

Then Gregorio grabbed Dario's shirt and pushed him hard. Dario stumbled, then fell sideways, into the path of an oncoming car. Valeria gasped and lurched towards him. Her fingers brushed his sleeve and closed on empty air. Brakes squealed. Then there was a terrifying thud as Dario fell headlong into the bonnet of the car.

Chapter 47

WORLDLY CHANGES

Valeria froze, hand still outstretched, then ran to where Dario lay on the ground. His body lay still. Too still. His eyes were glassy beneath half-open lids. A button was missing on his shirt. As the driver of the car rushed out, Valeria sank to the footpath. She was surely dreaming. This wasn't real. Dario would be okay. He had to be okay. He was strong. All would be okay.***

The driver knelt and pressed two fingers to Dario's neck. Valeria felt choked. The man stared at her strangely, but said nothing. Valeria waited, her voice like a stone in her throat.

He shook his head. "I'm sorry. He's dead."

No, No, it wasn't possible.

She hadn't spoken, but he answered her anyway. "He's not breathing. He's gone."

The world around her was spinning. Her chest pulled tight. Her body felt numb, disconnected from her head. She felt dizzy, weak, tired. She was dimly aware of people rushing around, screaming, of her own voice screaming, shouting, cursing, and her own hands pushing people away, as if by keeping them from Dario's body, she might somehow keep Death itself at bay. Alessandra had returned, but stood silent. She looked blurry.

Then strong hands pulled her back and held her close until her mind no longer absorbed anything. She slumped against a familiar solid chest, and as her world turned black, her nostrils filled with her father's smell of dirt and mint.

On the day of the funeral a few days later, the carabinieri showed up at her house. She sat on the bench while her family sat around the kitchen table, silent.

The policeman's dark uniform stood out as he took out a notepad. Another taller policeman stood alongside him, but turned his attention elsewhere. "We need to hear your side of the story to corroborate the statements of the witnesses."

Valeria nodded, an empty feeling in her stomach. Her hands clasped tightly in her lap. The ache in her chest felt like it might split her in two.

She drew in a deep breath and told him all she knew. After recounting the incident in detail, she added, "Dario lost his balance and—and—fell in front of that car. I told them to stop fighting, but they wouldn't listen. They wouldn't listen." She turned away, unable to stop the tears.

The policeman nodded. "The witnesses told me he wasn't purposely pushed on to the road. That it was an accident. Do you agree with that?"

Valeria shrugged. She didn't know anymore. The grief was scarring her soul. Would the pain ever stop? "I think so. He'd lost his balance and then couldn't control where he was going."

"We have had reports from some of the villagers about Gregorio's dealing with drugs. I'll need to speak to you about your knowledge of that. In the meantime, Gregorio has been advised to stay in the city, closer to where we can keep an eye on him, pending further investigation."

"Will Gregorio be arrested?"

The policeman cleared his throat as the taller officer spoke. "Pending further investigation, we'll possibly charge Gregorio for negligent homicide and possession of drugs. He won't be bothering you anymore."

Her mother rose from her seat in the kitchen. "Can this wait? We're not going anywhere. We'll answer your questions in the next couple of days about the drugs."

Her father put up his hand. "That's probably for the best, gentlemen."

The policemen hesitated, then nodded. "Alright. We'll be back to get your statement."

After the policemen left, her father sent the children to their rooms. "We need to talk to Valeria for a few minutes."

Valeria wiped away tears and swallowed. "What is it?"

Her parents sat beside her on the bench. Her mother held her hand and stroked her hair. A tear rolled down her mother's cheek.

"Darling, we're so sorry for your loss."

Valeria looked away. "Thanks, Mama."

Her mother bowed her head for a moment. "And we've come to the decision that staying here is probably not the best option."

Valeria's chest ached. "What do you mean?"

"There are so many sad memories here." Her mother closed her hand over Valeria's fingers. "How will you ever be happy? And—we just want you to be safe. Who knows how long Gregorio will be gone." She glanced towards Papa. Valeria knew Mama's concern was not entirely because of Gregorio.

Her father looked away as if he couldn't bear to see her grief. At least he wasn't yelling at her for being sad. He turned back to her. "Well, I've spoken to a friend of ours. Her nephew's living in Australia and likes it there. His name's Roberto and he's from a well-liked and trusted family," her father said.

An anxious feeling fluttered in her stomach. Where was this going?

Her father clasped his hands. "We'll be arranging for you to communicate with Roberto by mail.

Eventually you'll marry him and be a good wife to him."

Valeria was dumbstruck. She didn't know what to say. Why now? She had just lost Dario. There would never be another man for her. Never!

Yet, what kept her here now, apart from her family? She had lost the love of her life, and she doubted she'd find anyone as perfect as Dario. He would be her one, true love forever. Now he was gone, and she'd never see him again. She would miss his beautiful eyes, the way he laughed, his deep voice, and the gentle way he'd held and kissed her. She ached and longed for him, and that emptiness would never leave her. All she could move on to was to a life with a man she didn't love. She'd do her duty but that was all it would be. Obligation.

Mama leaned forward and laid a hand on Valeria's knee. "So, darling. How do you feel about that?"

Valeria shrugged, focusing her eyes on the ground.

"I know you're still grieving for your friend, and we don't expect you to leave now. Most likely in the next year or two." Her mother gave her a reassuring smile. "You don't have to worry about it now, darling. You're still far too young to travel to the other side of the world. When you're eighteen, you'll be ready."

She looked past her parents. "That's fine. Whatever you say." Valeria rose and walked into her bedroom, ignoring the stares of her sisters. With a shove by Carla, Elena left, and Valeria was left alone with her oldest sister.

Carla headed over to her bed. "Are you okay?"

Valeria blinked back tears. "Not really."

Carla leaned in and wrapped her arms around Valeria. "I'm so sorry, but it will get easier each day. We're all here for you, Valeria. You have our support."

In spite of Carla's kind words, Valeria felt nothing. She'd probably never feel anything ever again.

Chapter 48

LOOSE ENDS TIED UP (Two Years Later - 1965)

C rowds at the Leonardo da Vinci-Fiumicino Airport bustled about. Voices over a loudspeaker calling out flights unnerved Valeria while her family stood beside her. She struggled to cope with the noise, the chaos, the suitcases lingering and moving about as she waited at her gate to board the Alitalia flight to Australia. She sat on the padded seats, feeling comfortable in her black shift dress, a matching jacket, and cheap flat shoes given to her by her mother.

People kept coming and going as she stared around her. She smiled at Elena, Emilio, Carla, Maurizio, Giovanna, and her mother who were seated at the gate. She'd said goodbye to her father at home, as he'd mentioned having errands to do on the farm. A twinge in her stomach told her she didn't mind so much that he stayed back. He'd hurt her so much over the years. She still loved her father but she'd grown tired of his ways and his anger, and was better off living apart from him.

Valeria had said goodbye to Alessandra at her house. Her friend preferred not to come to the airport, saying that goodbyes were too hard. Valeria would deeply miss her friend, and promised to write her letters often. Valeria was warmed by the fact that Alessandra and Ciro were together and talking about marriage.

As for her mother and siblings, she'd miss all of them. It tugged at her heart that she'd be leaving them behind for many years. Maybe she would return for a visit one day.

Giovanna approached and sat next to her. "You look lovely, dear."

She turned to the old woman. "Thank you."

Giovanna brushed her hair away from her eyes, pondering. "And I'm so sorry about what Gregorio did to you."

She shook her head. "It's okay, Giovanna. You've been apologising for two years. It wasn't your fault."

"I don't care. I wanted you to know that he didn't mean to hurt your friend. It was an accident, but I couldn't say that at the time. You were grieving."

Valeria nodded. "How is Gregorio these days?"

"He's out of jail but he's gone to the city to live with his sister. He seems to be getting help from a doctor over there. He's found a job as a carpenter."

Valeria forced a smile. She still felt bitter towards Gregorio, but she had to let that go and forgive him. Dario's death was an accident, and he'd be forever in her heart. For her to move forward, she had to put it to the back of her mind and let it go.

Giovanna rose, and Mama slid into the seat. She wrapped an arm around Valeria's shoulder. "I am going to miss you so much, Valeria. Please write to us often, and maybe one day you can come visit." She turned away to hide the shimmer of tears. "And please be happy with Roberto. He's a good man."

Valeria's chest tightened, and her eyes welled. "I'll miss you too, Mama. I want you to be happy, and know that I'll always be thinking of you." She turned to her sisters and brother, whose cheeks were wet too.

Her flight number to Australia was suddenly called out. Valeria rose and grabbed her bag.

"Be happy," Carla said as they hugged.

Maurizio gave her a tight squeeze. "I hope you have a nice life with Roberto."

Her hand shook. "Thanks. I'll try."

Valeria embraced Elena next. "Send me some books from Australia when you come visit or you can post them," Elena said.

"I'll do that."

Emilio leaned in and wrapped his arms tightly around her. "I'll miss you, Valeria."

"I'll miss you too. Be brave."

She kissed Giovanna on the cheek, then rushed into her mother's arms.

"You write to us," Mama said again. "I love you so much, my darling."

"I love you too. All of you. Take care!"

As she made her way to the seat across the tarmac, it started to rain. Droplets of rain were not a bad thing, depending on how you looked at it. She remembered her mother's words a while back. "It's just like dancing in the rain. You'll always win out in the end. There will always be rain, dear one. We can choose to stay inside and cry about it, or we can go outside and dance. I believe you will choose to dance. Always remember that, Valeria." She did a little half-skip, trying it out. She could make the most of the rain or the sunshine, believing that she was on a journey to new adventures.

Reviews are gold to authors and allow Lucy to keep writing. If you enjoyed this story, please consider rating and reviewing it here: https://books2read.com/u/bOr7LA

Check out the future of Roberto's life with Valeria (The Italian Family Series) in *A New Life (FREE Novella)*: https://books2read.com/u/mqqwZm

Read more books in the Italian Family Series:

The Beauty of Tears:
https://books2read.com/u/bpqwk3

A Life By Design:
https://books2read.com/u/3J8ene

ABOUT THE AUTHOR

Lucy Appadoo is a prolific reader and author of the Friends In Crisis and Women Of Strength Series. After a childhood spent reading and imagining escapist worlds, Lucy has put her imagination into stories. Her work as a rehabilitation counsellor, and former work as a counsellor in private practice, have led to an interest in writing inspirational stories about authentic, driven women who manage adversity with strength and heart. She writes in the genres of romantic suspense/thrillers with significant life themes and contemporary romance.

Lucy's interests include researching crime stories and news to inspire her work, watching crime thrillers and suspenseful movies, travel, exercising, reading for entertainment or knowledge, meditation, and spending time with friends and family. She also appreciates her Italian background and culture, which has inspired her to write imaginative stories about her parents' childhoods, leading to The Italian Family Series novels.

Check out Lucy's website and sign up for a FREE book:

https://www.lucyappadooauthor.com.au

ALSO BY LUCY APPADOO

Web Of Lies (Book 3):

https://books2read.com/u/3JXazE
Love-Obsessed (Book 4):

https://books2read.com/u/4jPKGX

The Hearts Series – Romantic Suspense
Rising Hearts (Book 1):

https://books2read.com/u/mZwpoE
Forbidden Hearts (Book 2):

https://books2read.com/u/bQBKr7
Kindred Hearts (Book 3):

https://books2read.com/u/4AJKQK
Broken Hearts (prequel to Forbidden Hearts):

https://books2read.com/u/mgrnOD

Short Story Thrillers
Evening Interrupted:

https://books2read.com/u/3yZDjZ
The Dreamcatcher:

https://books2read.com/u/bzaLxn

Red Flags: https://books2read.com/u/bWZ9W1
Collection of Short Story Thrillers:

https://books2read.com/u/bP5vwj

The Italian Family Series - Coming of Age
Family Drama/Romance

A New Life: https://books2read.com/u/mqqwZm
The Beauty of Tears:

https://books2read.com/u/bpqwk3
A Life By Design: https://books2read.com/u/3J8ene

NON-FICTION
Grief & Loss
Moving Beyond Grief - How To Shift
From Grief & Loss to Joy & Peace:

https://books2read.com/u/mVNzDA

Stress Management & Anxiety
Holistic Spiritual and Mental Health -
Building Resilience and Creativity by
Conquering Anxiety and Managing Stress:

https://books2read.com/u/47kG8A

Career Guidance
Your Holistic Career Path - Create Career
Change, Satisfaction, and Work/Life Balance:

https://books2read.com/u/bzYDz4